THE NAKED TRUTH

The Confederation Treaty Book 2

LILLY CAIN

Lilly Cain

The Naked Truth

Tough. Capable. Most likely to survive anything. That's what they said about me in the past. But after I was captured and tortured, I'm a liability. After all, who could survive that and not break. Me, that's who, but no one trusts me and now I've been sent to the aliens for another round of questioning. But I won't crumble. I am Captain Susan Branscombe of the Starforce Marines.

How can I not feel for this strange woman? Her courage is undeniable and her strength impressive, even compared to an Inarrii. But my place it to find the truth, always the truth. Though her pain calls my soul to protect her, and my physical response to her is intense, I must know the truth, all of it. The role of Advocate Examiner for the humans is a heavy weight but I, Asler Kiis, will discover if this woman is a traitor.

Humans and Inarrii. Are they at war before a treaty can even be formed? Or is there another enemy? Only together can they find the answers.

Part Two of the Confederacy Treaty

The Naked Truth
The Confederation Treaty Series Book 2

Lilly Cain

ISBN 978-1-989138-03-8

Cover design by Candace Phillips Gilmer
Flirtation Designs

Discover other titles by Lilly Cain www.lillycain.com

To my mom who can no longer read or call me by name, but who loves me still.

Chapter 1

"Fuckitall," Captain Susan Branscombe slurred as she woke to the sound of gunfire and running footsteps. She lay on the cold floor of an empty storage room; only the light from the force bindings on her arms and legs provided any illumination. She shivered then groaned in pain as the trembling motion brought cramps to her arms and legs. If they didn't unbind her and let her up soon, she wouldn't be able to walk.

She grimaced in the darkness. Even that tiny motion sent waves of pain across her face and down her neck. She wasn't sure she'd be able to walk anyway after the last beating.

Susan could taste blood in her mouth. The coppery tang would have made her wretch if she hadn't strictly controlled herself. She wasn't certain how badly she was injured – one wound on her leg seeped and bled where she'd been burned, and her arm was definitely broken, along with several fingers. Dried blood caked on one cheek pulled as she grimaced, and her head throbbed. *How bad is my face?* They'd cut off her hair and sliced her cheek and nose.

Before she could begin to pity herself, the floor heaved in a sudden explosion.

They were under attack. Not surprising. She'd told them the way to the base and now she would die, along with the terrorists that held her captive. At least she could end it knowing her fellow Starforce Marines would defeat them. They were a kick-ass bunch, every one of them, and she was damn proud to be among them, even if this was how it ended.

Another booming explosion threw her against the wall of the tiny room. *This is it.* Soon the walls of the ship would rip open, and she would die in the cold void of space. *Thank God.* She was so tired of pain; death would be welcome. She waited, but a final explosion didn't come. Instead the room grew even blacker. She realized she was losing consciousness and fought against it.

Sue flinched as bright beams of light swept across the room and over her. A blurred face appeared before her, and rough hands reached out to grab roughly at the lapels of her ruined uniform.

"Get it over with, asshole," she ground out through pain. She resisted as she was lifted, but the blackness returned and stole away the last of her defiance.

CONFEDERACY EXAMINER ASLER KIIS sat at the large oval conference table and listened with waning patience to the chaos around him. His long robes, although of the softest *chammiss* available, were heavy and irritating. The drone of constant chatter from the ongoing conference was also annoying, and the reason for calling the conference even more so. He tapped his fingers against the polished walnut surface of the table, admiring its quality and the striking pattern of the unique Earth product even as he planned his next move.

As Lead Examiner during the mission to contact the human race, he was also Examiner Advocate for the Earth people until such a time as the first treaty between the

Confederacy and the humans was complete. Whether the humans knew it or not, he was there to protect and defend them.

Of course, should the need arise he was also there to judge and punish as necessary. It was the highest position he'd achieved to date, and the most honor his clan had garnered in three generations. He was the youngest Examiner to achieve Advocate position in a hundred years, and he wasn't about to lose the chance to make history.

His entourage of fellow officers and Co-Examiner, Salis Fiiten, sat with him on one side of the table. All waited silently as the members of Earth's Starforce Marines argued among themselves on the other side. Or, at least some of them argued. Top Admiral Jeffers and Base Commander Davies sat as silently as the Confederacy team. These were the men to watch.

In many ways, Earth people were not dissimilar to his own, Asler thought, but most humans lacked the ability to touch each other as his people did, mind to mind. Perhaps this was why they were so loud and argued so much. Maybe if he had been older than his thirty years—maybe if he had been as aged as his predecessor—he could have continued to wait while the humans fought it out. But he wasn't.

"Enough," he echoed the thought aloud to Salis. Silently he mind-spoke to him. *No more wasting time. Tell Admiral Jeffers we have made our decision, and if Earth wishes to begin Treaty talks with us, we must, and will, have control over this investigation into the attack.*

As he spoke the words into the mind of his partner, he stood, bringing the attention of the room back to him and his silent officers. In the first days of the initial treaty talks a vicious attack had damaged both Inarrii and human starships. The Confederacy demanded a measure of control over the investigation into the attack, an investigation which the humans seemed determined to handle alone. The argument, not the first of its kind, had raged for the last half-hour of Earth time, monopolized by the Earth military. It was not going to continue.

Salis, rising with his co-Examiner, explained once again that the Confederacy would conduct the investigation or would break off the treaty discussions.

Immediately several voices broke into heated argument. One caught Asler's attention—grizzled Earth Starforce Base Commander Davies, who until this moment had sat silently at the admiral's side.

"Captain Branscombe must be excused from any investigation!" the base commander demanded. His face was flushed and his words ripped through the clamor. "She's suffered enough at the hands of these terrorists," he insisted. "There is no reason to believe she had anything to do with this attack. She's been tortured, for Christ's sake."

"She may very well have been forced to give up the location of the base," interjected a young man. Asler had determined the speaker was a Starforce Lieutenant by his insignia and likely to be an Earth lawyer of some sort. The position was not one that Asler's race employed; with Examiners there could be no doubt when truth was determined, and therefore there was no need to argue over motivation, or punishment.

"Or perhaps she gave it up willingly after being with them this long," insisted another officer.

The argument had been heard before. What caught Asler's ear was the sincerity and concern ringing behind the base commander's words. The sentiments were echoed in his emotional projection. Obviously the old man cared for the woman as if she was his own child. The base commander's rage over her treatment and his fear over what might happen to her at the hands of the alien Confederacy tugged at Asler's heart. While Asler wouldn't enter another's mind uninvited, this man's emotions rose and pushed past the barriers of his mind and overflowed clearly into the room.

Asler's beliefs would never allow an innocent to be

mistreated, but he had to make a demonstration of the Confederacy's power. The two compulsions pulled at him, and his head throbbed in reaction. There were factions on Earth that believed the Confederacy should leave, that for humans to work with aliens was an abomination. Their voices were a force, albeit a small one, in the human media.

As an Examiner, Asler knew his duty was to prove the Confederacy's strength by finding answers, and then to quickly mete out punishment where it was due. Perhaps the woman was innocent, but having been found on the vessel that had attacked the first scheduled Treaty talks, he too had to wonder how much she had told, how much she had been involved. As a Starforce Marine pilot she knew enough to be dangerous in enemy hands.

He squared his shoulders. Above all, the truth must be revealed. He signaled his entourage of fellow officers and as a group they stood beside him and Salis, and turned to leave the room.

"Wait," a voice filled with command called to them.

Asler turned back, already hearing the capitulation tinged with frustration in the mind of the Starforce admiral. Asler noted the power in his strong shoulders belying the heavy creases in his face. This was a man accustomed to the weight of responsibility..

"Admiral Jeffers," Asler responded, his trained voice perfectly even, uninflected with any emotion.

"The investigation is yours. You'll have full access to all our databases and scans of what happened. A complete record will be beamed to you immediately."

"And the surviving prisoners - the captured Starforce officer?"

The admiral's lips thinned. He laid a hand on the shoulder of the base commander who had protested so strongly, calming him with a gesture not unlike one Asler would use in the same situation. "They're yours." He raised his other hand as his grip on Base Commander

Davies became stronger. "But you will consult us before any and all judgments are made."

Asler heard the iron in the admiral's voice, but he knew he had to be the stronger opponent in this confrontation. The Confederacy must have compliance. "You will not be involved in any judgment, Admiral. However, we will inform you before any punishments are meted out."

Asler turned and left as the protests began again behind him. His thoughts were grim as he walked quickly through the hallways of the Earth vessel toward his shuttle. It was doubtful this would be the last time the argument came up. Earth's people didn't trust the Confederacy yet— and how could they, really? They'd only been contacted a few months earlier. But if Earth was to be saved from pillaging by the larger universe, they must become part of the Confederacy. It was either that or be stripped of their resources by the pirates the Confederacy battled on a daily basis.

The more he interacted with Earth people like the admiral and the base commander, the more they seemed worth saving. But he needed data, needed to understand them better in order to fight for a decent treaty for them. Despite being the Examiner Advocate for Earth, even despite the fact that his clan relied on him and his current rank to bring them status, he knew himself well enough that if he didn't believe in his cause, he wouldn't argue as effectively as he could. Earth had resources that the Confederacy wanted—metals and organics like the fine wooden conference table, and most of all imaginative, intelligent and culturally diverse people. In return, the Confederacy could offer protection and technological advancement for the planet. A treaty would benefit everyone—Earth, the Confederacy, himself and even his clan, millions of light years away on their home planet Inarr. But he still wouldn't support the treaty without having faith in the people.

He'd met only one human on a personal level at this

point, not counting those attending the elaborate and lengthy treaty negotiations. Earth's Starforce Major David Brown had made first contact with the Inarrii—or rather, they had contacted him. Major Brown was a strong and commanding presence, a man Asler enjoyed meeting. He spoke easily and commanded the men in his squad of fighter pilots with care and integrity. He handled his new role as emissary with equal care. Brown's personality had played a big part in the willingness of Confederacy representatives, like Asler, to begin Treaty negotiations with Earth that would greatly favor the humans, although they were likely unaware of the fact as yet.

"If we find their officer guilty, they'll never trust us," Salis stated flatly into Asler's mind. He paused in front of the entrance as the security scanner took his genetic imprint for comparison.

"They may not." Asler mentally replied. *"We'll know soon enough."*

Entering the softly lit shuttle, Asler felt immediate relief from the tension he'd suffered onboard the Earth vessel. There were too many unshielded people there, too many untempered emotions as people wondered about the Confederacy's arrival and what it meant to them.

Salis groaned and pulled his robe over his head, shedding the heavy garment quickly. Around them, other officers stripped as well, pulling off the clothing deemed correct for meeting this new species. Asler followed suit, stripping down to his *pettan*, a short-legged covering that wrapped him loosely from his waist to just above his knee. Earlier members of the Confederacy sent to observe human behavior noted that the Earth people wore many layers of clothing and suggested that wearing just the *pettan* in public might be considered disrespectful.

Inarrii were the perfect first contacts for Earth—they were shaped much like humans, though somewhat more muscular and about a hand's-breadth taller than a human's average height. Only their *L'inar* truly set them apart in appearance, the curving sienna-colored nerve lines that covered their skin from under their hairline, down the back of the neck and over most of their torso. There were many within the Confederacy who looked far more exotic. In some cases their appearance differed so much that humans might not accept them as friendly.

Asler lowered himself onto a low couch, letting the heat and vibrations from its cushions relax him further.

"Could I offer a calming moment, Examiner Kiis?" One of the female officers approached him. She reached her hand, palm forward to him, offering him as much comfort as he might desire in her arms. Physical touch kept the Inarrii calm and reduced the wear on their emotions caused by the psychic onslaught of close proximity to a species that did not shield their emotions. Sex was the common and often desired result.

Many of the younger officers were here for that reason, although the comfort would be shared by both participants. Behind her, Asler caught a glimpse of a grinning Salis shaking his head.

Asler stifled his own urge to smile. She was young and took her duties far too seriously.

"Thank you, but I'm about to review the investigation. The prisoner was badly injured, and I will need all my strength to deal with her. Perhaps Salis has some need to share with you."

She turned from him without any sign of rejection and made the suggestion to Salis. Now it was Asler who shook his head as his partner immediately took her up on her offer, a wicked grin spreading across his face as he led her away.

Asler's smile ended abruptly. He hadn't lied; he never would. Inarrii believed in truth, Examiners even more so. He knew the Starforce officer had been badly injured. She *would* need all his strength. He must discover what kind of threat the renegade forces that had attacked the first round of treaty talks represented; he must know if the attack was based on irrational fear of the unknown, a common enough problem for first encounters, or if it was something more dangerous.

If the treaty failed, so many of his efforts would be wasted. This one mission could make or break his future. While he had achieved much, his clan would still suffer as they had wagered a lot on his growing career. Anything that could stall or force the treaty to fail must be stopped. If the human Officer Branscombe knew anything, he would have to discover it.

THE LIGHTS WERE TOO BRIGHT. They kept her awake when all she wanted was to sleep. Worse, the Medtechs never left her alone, and were always prodding her, poking her with some needle or drawing blood or insisting she talk or eat.

She hurt everywhere. She didn't want to talk to them, hadn't expected to have to live long enough to have to tell them what she had gone through. She didn't want to think about it. What was done was done, no use crying about it.

"Captain Branscombe, open your eyes!" The sharp bark of her commander had her snapping to alertness even as part of her willed him to go away. The nasty vomit-green walls of the medroom swam into focus, along with the blinking lights of her medical monitors and her commander's concerned frown.

"Listen up, Branscombe, and pay attention. I know damn well you're a good soldier and loyal to the Starforce Marines. Never mind what they're saying. You stand tall and proud." Commander John Davies leaned over her, his grey camouflage hat seeming to blend in with his hair. Steel blue eyes stared into her own.

"The admiral has decided the Confederacy will be handling the investigation into the attack." He turned away from her, looking at the humming machines that surrounded her medroom bed. "It's not my choice, but you are to report to the Confederacy shuttle at o-nine-hundred today."

"What?" She struggled to sit up, tried to understand through the haze of drugs she'd been given what he was trying to say. "Am I under investigation?"

"I'll be frank, Branscombe. There are some who are certain you gave away the location of the base."

To hell with this. She lifted her chin and stared into his eyes. "I did."

"What?" He shook his head. "You were tortured. You didn't know what you were doing."

"I knew exactly what I was doing. I did tell them, but only because I fully expected our ships to defeat theirs. I knew if I didn't give them a believable target, they'd attack somewhere else, maybe some place we couldn't defend. We had three warships at the base, Commander. There was no chance we wouldn't win. That was the part I didn't tell them. It was the only thing I could do." Spent and dizzy from the longest speech she'd made since her rescue, she dropped back against the bed pillow.

"Hmmph," he huffed, his face unreadable.

A soft rustling noise at the doorway caught Sue's attention. Her eyes flicked to a stranger at the entrance and back to her base commander as he opened his mouth to say more.

"Captain Susan Branscombe, you are requested to accompany me to the Confederacy ship Horneu," the stranger spoke brusquely, interrupting Davies.

The base commander's mouth snapped shut. He swallowed whatever he had been about to say, looking as if the taste of it hit a sour note..

Sue examined the figure in her doorway, her gaze caught by the startlingly intense expression in the stranger's eyes. His mouth turned down at the corners, full lips pressed thin in a disapproving glance. She shivered, her fingers nervously fisting in the soft folds of the medroom bedcovers. *How long has he been listening?*

He had to be an Inarrii. She'd seen pictures, read the descriptions of all the aliens in the Confederacy they were about to join. She'd even had personal contact with Alinna Gaerrii, the Inarrii spy who'd practically crash-landed in her back yard. She'd guessed the Inarrii were selected from among the Confederacy to discuss the treaty because they would garner the most respect. They looked human, aside from their skin markings, which to her eye looked like henna tattoos.

What the pictures hadn't shown, or perhaps she hadn't noticed, was how patrician their features were, with their long, thin noses and well-defined cheekbones and jaws, sensual lips. She certainly hadn't noticed Alinna that way. And the news vids hadn't done justice to the gorgeous contrast of bronzed skin against dark hair and eyebrows, either. *Or how their bright green eyes could flash with anger.* Discomfort sent a chill through her as curiosity morphed into anxiety.

"Commander Davies, we do not need your presence, nor was it indicated or even implied that you would brief Captain Branscombe. Please leave." His voice was tight with controlled emotion, but she could see it reflected in his eyes.

Sue watched as her base commander drew himself up, his spine snapping stiffly to full attention. This was the man she'd come to consider as a friend, perhaps even a father, in light of her orphaned state. She'd served under him for nearly a dozen years, on one base or another until her recent transfer to the Mars Settlement Defense unit. And when that mission had been placed on hold with the Confederacy's arrival, she'd returned to piloting the base scout shuttle at his request. Now he defended her again, even though she'd disappointed him and her career was likely over. She tasted bitterness at the realization. She'd never fly again, and her dream of visiting an alien world only that, an impossible dream.

"Examiner Kiis. Dragging this woman out of her sick bed is ridiculous. I can't imagine what you hope to accomplish, but this kind of behavior won't go unnoticed," Davies said coldly.

The Inarrii stepped into the room, his shadow stretching over Sue as she lay on the medroom bed. Her heart pounded. He was taller than the commander. Not by much, but he seemed huge from her vulnerably prone position. She pressed backward against the pillow, but there was nowhere to go.

Her mouth dried as the stranger broke eye contact with the base commander and looked down at her. This was an Examiner, one of the Confederacy law enforcement officials.

What the hell does he want with me? What is he going to do with me? Interrogate me? Torture me some more?

A shudder rippled down her spine, despite her attempts to stay calm. She ground her teeth together. *Get it together Branscombe, tough it out.*

Chapter 2

It was worse than he'd imagined. Fear and aggression radiated from the woman on the bed. The captain was far more injured than he had been led to believe, damaged in both mind and body. Unmistakable feelings of panic and pain projected toward him—she feared him. Damn the base commander for telling her anything. Now she presumed him to be antagonistic, and given the recent torture she had endured, he could well imagine what treatment she would expect from him. This would make her interrogation much harder. He corrected himself internally. It would make her healing harder and her questioning brutal.

"Commander Davies, you are dismissed," Asler stated flatly, never taking his eyes off the injured woman.

"Just how do you intend to take her to your ship in this condition, Kiis?" Commander Davies scoffed. "We don't even want to move her to the base."

Asler noted the woman's heartbeat increased at the mention of being taken away, and her eyes darted to the commander. Her lips pressed together tightly in her pale face. Her short cropped hair, in a shade of frosty blonde that only humans could achieve naturally, matched her creamy skin—a tone that seemed to be nearing the white of her bandages. The terrorists had slashed one cheek, high on her prominent cheekbone, and sliced the edge of her pert nose. Even her eyes had not gone unscathed. One of her dark blue eyes, so huge in her face as she looked at him, sported a bruise nearly the same color as her iris.

He took stock of her other injuries. His mind lightly brushed her subconscious to gather the information without intruding: burns, broken arm, four broken fingers, more cuts, bruises, exhaustion, malnourishment, and possible minor internal damage.

The physical damage would have to be taken care of before the mental could truly be assessed. Her subconscious was hiding damage from her. She did not want to face what had been done to her. That might make a true determination of her involvement with the terrorists the most difficult of all the truths he must determine.

Suddenly aware that he had been standing there for several minutes, staring at the injured officer—nearly touching her—Asler shook his head. He extended his hand and touched her forehead, quickly dropping her into a light dream-free level of rest. Dreams were another area he would deal with onboard the Horneu.

As he removed his hand, Base Commander Davies made a muted sound of protest.

"The medical team onboard will heal her before any questioning begins. We are not a culture that includes pain in our interrogations." He glanced over at the commander and offered Davies the only comfort he could, his word that his charge would not be tortured. He must keep a completely indifferent façade in front of the Earth personnel, despite what he felt from them and for them. The Confederacy must be in control.

Tapping his wrist sensor, Asler signaled the medical team he was on his way back with a patient. A second tap activated the transfer bubble, a device not allowed to be used on Earth until this moment.

"Step back, Commander." Asler gathered up the unconscious woman, ignoring the various cords and tubes attached to her body.

The bubble formed around them, visible to the naked eye. It enveloped them and enlarged to surround the officer's sick-bed and monitors, crowding the commander to the doorway. The bubble began to gain in opalescent color, and Asler watched in mild amusement as the base commander's jaw dropped open in surprise. Visibly new technology provided a good reminder why the Earth people needed the Confederacy. But his humor died as he took in the man's fear for the woman Asler held in his arms.

With an inaudible yet tangible snap of power, the bubble transferred its contents to the Horneu's medical facility. As the phase completed, he found himself somewhat reluctant to release the woman from his arms and give her into the hands of the medical team.

Again he shook his head at himself. He must remain in control. His naturally protective instincts must be put on hold. He was an Examiner, and the mission depended on his ability to keep his emotions and hers separate from the search for truth.

THERE WAS NO MORE PAIN. *I'm dreaming. If I open my eyes, I'll be awake again; it will hurt again.* Sue sighed. Velvety softness cocooned her body, held her in a warm embrace. Even her face seemed enfolded in some supple material, muting all other sensations.

For the first time in a long time she felt safe, protected as though someone held her in their arms. As if she wasn't alone. She reveled in the feeling in a way she would never reveal to anyone. She was a Starforce Marine pilot, after all. But for one moment she could take pleasure in the comfort.

"Damn. If only I didn't have to pee." Her lips brushed something as she spoke. She struggled to sit up but the covering material resisted. She opened her eyes to blackness and began to struggle in earnest to escape, kicking out against whatever held her. Her sense of comfort evaporated. Cold fear pushed a clammy sweat to her forehead.

Immediately she found herself immobilized, unable to even cry out in the outrage and fear that suddenly possessed her.

Where the hell was she?

"Captain Branscombe, please hold still," commanded a deep voice.

As soon as she complied the pressure holding her in place eased. The coverings began to pull away, and Sue sucked in a deep shuddering breath as she took stock. The pressure restraining her lessened further. She still felt no pain—it hadn't been a dream. Her arm could move, the fingers flex.

Despite the warning to be still, she stretched and shifted inside the wrapping. The pain really was gone, her arm no longer broken. Even her left bicep contracted without pulling, the scar from her old laser burn gone. Scarring she knew could never disappear.

Her mind recoiled. She'd been completely healed. She must therefore be on the alien ship, mended by some strange technology. *To what end? So they can torture me all over again? Or patch me up so I can stand trial without the badges of torture plain to any who see me?*

Finally the coverings across her eyes were lifted. He was there, the alien Examiner Kiis. How odd that someone whose name sounded so intimate, like the touch of a lovers lips, would now be her tormenter. She fought to keep her breathing steady. Beyond that, if she looked at only his face, at those finely chiseled cheekbones and bright green eyes, he looked sensual enough to match his name. Exotic tattoos ran along the edge of his jawbone and down his neck, forming an amazing swirl of bronze-colored patterns. The designs were mesmerizing.

She swallowed hard and slowly stretched again. *Do not go there, ever. Handsome interrogators can be just as cruel as the uglies.*

"Move slowly," he instructed. "You've been healing for over forty-eight of your hours."

She sat up. Prudence would have had her moving slowly anyway, but caution imposed by a stranger standing over her drove the point home. She could feel his eyes on her, staring with that focused glare.

She clenched her teeth together. Never in her life had she feared a stranger. Not until the pain…she thrust the thought from her mind, refusing to think about what had been done to her. As she levered herself against what seemed to be a mattress of some sort, the now loose covers revealed she was naked. She grabbed them tightly to her as they slipped and nearly exposed one breast.

"Ahh…" she cleared her throat and tried again, glancing around the strange room. She would get through this. These were not the people who had hurt her. To her left stood another Inarrii, this one calmly fiddling with what she took to be medical equipment. She nodded to the light-grey garbed Medtech and addressed him, "Thanks for the patch job. I didn't feel a thing."

The Medtech smiled at her. "You'll have to thank Examiner Kiis, as well. His skill with perception is why you experienced no pain during your healing."

"Thanks anyway. You even ditched my laser scar." Sue groaned inwardly. *Kiis is talented in twisting perception.* The aliens had already been messing with her brain. *Wonderful.* She swallowed as the realization hit her. She really hadn't been alone.

She glanced back at Kiis. *Why does he have to stand so damn close?* "Thank you. But let's get this over with. What do you want? Why am I here? Why did you bother to heal me?"

"I will ask the questions, Captain Branscombe," his deep voice rumbled, sending a quick shiver down her spine. "You will come with me."

"I need clothes." In truth, she hadn't felt a need for modesty for the last several years in the force; there wasn't room for it in the tight quarters of the Starforce spaceships. But to be naked now—in front of an alien who had already touched her mind—made her mouth suddenly dry. Trying to remind herself again that these were not the people who'd held her so cruelly wasn't working. Even her knowledge that her last commander, Major David Brown, had fallen in love with one of them wasn't enough to calm her racing heart.

He looked at her for a moment and then opened a small cupboard she hadn't noticed, located to one side of the medbed. He pulled out some sort of material and handed it to her.

"May I have some privacy?" she asked tightly.

He crossed his arms and remained staring at her.

A flush of embarrassment travelled from her cheeks to her throat and downward. *Lovely.* Lips pressed tightly together, she unfolded the garment – the slippery material difficult to manipulate with one hand as her other gripped the bedcovers. "What the hell is this? It's only frikkin half here. Where the top?"

"It is a *pettan.* You will see most of our crew wearing these while you are here. If it isn't good enough for you, we will request a shipsuit."

"What I'd like is my own uniform." She eyed him. *He certainly isn't wearing one of these little things.*

"You will get dressed now, or come along unclothed."

He isn't kidding. Her initial incredulousness wavered now between embarrassment, anger and, she admitted to herself, fear. *So the torture begins with humiliation.* That thought had her dropping her grip on the bedcovers and moving to yank on the offensive garment. Damned if she'd let anyone get the better of her over such a stupid little thing.

Unfortunately, her sudden movements brought on a wave of dizziness. She lost her balance, tilting into Kiis.

He caught her, his long-fingered hands grasping her naked shoulders. Skin to skin, they froze. She glanced up, into those incredibly bright green eyes. The medical facility faded. They were in darkness, a darkness she remembered, feared. The scent of rusted metal, dried blood. The deafening silence punctured only by the creaking groans of the outer wall of the decrepit old ship.

"No!" She pulled away from him, terror wrenching her away from the past and catapulting her right back into the present, where the lights of the medical facility appeared thankfully bright. "What the hell was that?" her voice quavered, and she hated herself for the weakness it revealed.

"Please." The deep timbre of his voice registered softly, his voice suddenly gentle. "Come with me."

She sucked in a breath and turned her back on him, finished pulling on the *pettan*. The material reminded her of her favorite silk nightie, one she'd had for years. She thought about that as she dressed, thought about anything other than the darkness she'd just faced. She concentrated on her breathing, the lights, the sounds, even Kiis's suddenly comforting presence.

The thought pulled her up short. *Be a Marine, woman!*

She straightened; her breasts seemed to sit on display. She gritted her teeth. "I think I'd like that shipsuit," she told him, keeping her back to him. Her nipples had peaked. The weight of her breasts, not something she would normally notice given that she was at most an average size, seemed exaggerated without something to cup them to her body.

She turned to face him. She stifled a groas as she realized that once again her embarrassment had made its presence known in a very physical way. The flush on her cheeks probably reached the tips of her bare nipples, although she refused to check the fact. She had to tilt her head up to look him in the eye. She was a tall woman, but the Inarrii male had a good six inches on her. Despite that, she couldn't miss the way his eyes roamed over her body. She shivered in response. Things were changing and moving too fast.

She fisted her hands in frustration. She *was* a Marine, but she'd gone from expecting to die, to being accused of God knew what, to being miraculously healed. Then in a blink of an eye she faced semi-naked captivity, flashbacks, and a captor who made no sense at all.

Kiis turned from her, began to move toward the exit. She had no choice but to follow him. A small part of her mind occupied itself with examining the strange ship for any way of escape. But the larger part of her mind shut that down—she didn't know what half the equipment around her might be for, let alone how it worked. Even the walls appeared odd, shapes and colors showing faintly on the surface and changing as she stepped nearer. She didn't know where she was or even if the ship was anywhere near Earth.

Besides, she was innocent. The Inarrii were supposed to be the good guys. She hadn't really done anything wrong. Sure she had given out information, but not enough to ensure that the terrorists would win; just enough that they would lose. And she had been under duress…incredible duress and pain.

But I am never thinking about that again.

ASLER SENSED the flow of emotion behind him. She trailed him through the corridors toward his quarters. That she followed him despite her apprehension was a very good sign. It meant that on some level she accepted him as an authority, as she would her own military superiors. This was exactly the reason he'd made an effort to be firm about her attire matching those around her onboard the Inarrii ship. Maybe she wouldn't like him or really trust him, but she would understand she needed to obey him. It marked the beginning of the end of her fear. Her physical healing had helped that as well.

As they walked, Asler reflected on their first contact. Grabbing her to stop her fall had been completely accidental, but it had immediately opened mental contact between them. Because he was the directing force and had been thinking of her torture, her mind had taken them to the place and time of her capture. But she had shut it down. *Surprising.* She had the power to close out his guidance, at least on a primitive level. It might make things easier if she had some ability, or it could actually make things much harder. That remained to be seen.

"Ah, this is the prisoner, then?" Salis and one of the security staff stepped out of an adjoining corridor. As usual, his thoughts contained a hint of mockery. Not for the first time, Why the man continued to serve when nothing in the Confederacy ever truly seemed to please him was a mystery. Everything and anything might become the target of his sarcastic brand of humor.

Although he had always been a friend, Asler wished Salis had chosen another time to approach the human officer. The Inarrii officer accompanying Salis didn't seem too happy with his distraction either. It felt, from the disgruntled emotions emanating from her, as though the two of them had been about to engage in the one other thing Salis enjoyed—sex.

"She's rather pretty. Perhaps this treaty will have more rewards than a boost to your career."

"Perhaps you should be on your way. I believe your friend won't wait for you much longer." Asler paused at the corner of the hallway to his quarters. Salis would give up in a moment. He really wasn't a bad person, and he would sense the human's residual fear. He just couldn't stop teasing and

taunting, using his twisted humor to mask his own personal demons.

The security officer, a tall, strong-looking female with three unusually noticeable scars across her upper arm, stepped toward Officer Branscombe, her curiosity clear in her dark green eyes. Asler helt the human stiffen beside him, her anxiety palpable. When the Inarrii reached out and ran a finger over the smooth skin of her arm, Captain Branscombe knocked her hand aside.

"She might be pretty if she wasn't so smooth. You might have to work hard to get a response from this one, Kiis," Salis joked.

"She has no *l'inar?*" The woman spoke aloud, her security clearance clearly having given her more than a cursory knowledge of human language. Her curiosity's sharp edge cut through the air.

Asler remembered then—this was the officer who had been wounded in the terrorist attack. Her *l'inar* had been cut along one arm, a serious injury that rendered the nerve lines on the woman's appendage useless until she completed a lengthy series of healings, perhaps lasting for years, if they were able to heal at all. "Sergeant Sarina Tariim, this is Captain Susan Branscombe."

Tariim's face hardened as she realized who the human must be. She took a step toward Branscombe, but the human stood her ground. Asler watched carefully and noted Salis doing the same. What happened next would be a revealing event for the character of both women. No doubt Salis was caring for Tariim after her injury.

"Did you do it? Did you bring the attack down on us?" Tariim growled at the human.

"I didn't do anything. I don't even know who they are. The bastards did their best to kill me." Branscombe said nothing further, but her posture spoke for her as she clenched her fists and thrust out her jaw.

"But you did lead them to us." Tariim crowded her, pressing the issue, clearly looking for someone to blame.

"You were strong enough to beat them off. Not

everyone they might have attacked could have done it. Would you rather they struck at the civilians?"

"*Enough. Stand down Tariim. Salis, see to your charge.*" Asler stepped between the women, the move as surprising to himself as much as to the others. He could see the shock in Salis's usually guarded expression. Tariim was a dangerous physical opponent, and Examiners did not risk their talents by engaging in violent disagreements.

"*He is not my keeper. I am fine.*" Without waiting for a response Tariim strode away, her back stiff and the *l'inar* ridging along her back and shoulders.

Branscome said nothing, her eyes darting from one Inarrii to the next. He wondered at her silence, but didn't miss the way she'd slid into a fighting stance, turning her back to the wall of the corridor.

Salis made a small negating gesture, his emotions actively promoting calm in a way even the captain could likely feel. "My apologies, Captain Branscombe. I didn't realize how this chance meeting would affect Officer Tariim. As you may have guessed, she was injured in the terrorist attack." Salis bowed and left them, his path the same as the one Tariim had taken.

Asler waited until they turned the corner of the hallway then apologized to Branscombe. "I am sorry about that. It is clear that Examiner Salis is treating Sergeant Tariim for emotional pain and expected that a confrontation with someone she blames for her injury would help her in some way."

Branscombe straightened. "Whatever." She stared at the floor, her jaw clenched as she tried to deny the effect Tariim's accusations had on her. "I'm sorry she was injured," she muttered.

He sensed the emotion behind her spare words. She meant it. More, she respected Tariim, as if she had spoken with an equal rather than an antagonist.

"Come, we are almost there." He considered the truth of her last statement as they walked the length of the hallway. Just because she was sorry an individual was injured didn't mean she hadn't committed the act. And yet instinctively he had protected her. His instincts were not something he could afford to ignore.

They reached the entry to his quarters. He stopped, giving the security scanner a moment to recognize him. Captain Branscombe came close, but avoided bumping into his back.

"Every entrance is protected by security scan," he told her without turning.

The door slid open, retracting into the wall, and he stepped inside. The first room acted as both social sitting area and office and included two long low benches, each wide and long enough for two people to stretch out together. His command console was mounted into a workstation, and there wasn't much more. He hadn't personalized the space—this mission had been assigned to him at the last moment when his predecessor, Examiner Kintaar, had been killed in the line of duty—so the walls remained a blank canvas.

He strode toward a bench but changed his mind at the last moment and settled down at the workstation, a position of more authority.

The captain entered the space slowly and sat on the edge of the bench nearest to the door. She didn't say anything. He watched her eyes darting about the room, taking in the darkened doorway to his sleeproom and the second exit to his private lavatory. Her hands gripped the edge of the bench cushion, but her spine remained stiff. He silently cheered her on—applauding her bravery after her recent ordeal. She would heal.

"Captain Branscombe, you have been implicated in the recent attack on the Confederacy. As you know, you are now under investigation regarding what information, exactly, you gave to the terrorist group Terran Purity, and under what conditions." He stated it flatly, laying the situation out for her. "All investigations in this matter are being conducted by the Confederacy. Treason," he paused, looking at her pale face, "can carry a penalty as severe as execution."

"Sir—"

He interrupted her with a raised hand. "I am here to determine the truth, and to defend or prosecute you as necessary. It is in your best interest to cooperate with me completely."

"I have every intention of doing that," she said through clenched teeth.

"I assure you, we do not use torture." He watched her take that in, absorb it. "But I will know, absolutely, if you lie in any way or attempt to hide information." He rose, walked to her. "You will show me every moment of your time with the terrorists."

"Show you?" She didn't look away from him, but he could tell she wanted to as her shoulders tilted slightly away.

"When I touched you in the medroom, you flashed back to your cell on the terrorist ship."

"Yes..." she breathed. "Oh, no...you don't mean..."

He watched as realization dawned on her. "Yes. I can be there in your mind, with you. Inarrii have the ability, as I believe you may know, to speak telepathically. Examiners can do more, we can walk through memories with others, including humans. All it requires is a touch."

She wet her lips. Her face had paled again. He watched tiny bumps flash down the length of her skin as fear set in once again. It was an amazing reaction, one his kind didn't have. He looked closer and saw that tiny hairs on her bare arms and breasts had risen, causing the bumps from her anxiety. His gaze slid only a little further. Her chest heaved as she took an alarmed breath, and her nipples hardened.

He brushed a hand over the taught skin of her bicep, along the sensual curve of her shoulder to rest on the back of her neck. Her eyes had grown huge, the pupils dilated to the point where they nearly hid the dark blue of her irises.

"Don't touch me," she whispered harshly.

"I must. We must know the truth, Captain Branscombe."

Blackness bloomed between them. She shuddered as the scent of rusting metal, blood, and stale urine filtered through their shared senses. He admired her more as he recognized her internal struggle. She fought the desire to retreat, to wrench herself free of his touch. But her determination won out, at least for the moment, and he examined the dark walls surrounding them.

"Where are we?" He tested their contact with the question.

"This is it. This is the room I woke up in when they first took down my shuttle. I was scouting the perimeter but they took out my shields and laser before I even good a good look at them."

"Had you met any of them before?" Asler whispered into her mind.

"No." Her mental voice seemed strained but only from fear. There was no way to lie here, mind to mind. She could say untrue words but they wouldn't match her memories, or her emotions.

"You weren't hurt?"

"No, not by the attack. Not yet."

Shadows shifted in the darkness. Muted sounds of approaching feet had her cringing, the reaction enough to ignite his sympathy. He pulled her into his arms. A metallic squeal preceded a blinding light as the door to the dank room opened. Hands reached for her, grabbed at her, tried to tear her away from him. He held on but the mental contact was broken.

Asler opened his eyes, met her gaze. They were pressed together, lying back now on the wide couch. One arm held her tightly to him, his other hand splayed across one of her pert little breasts. Physical contact made the reading very personal, and absolutely accurate. He must have physically embraced her as they moved into her memory, just as he had mentally on the terrorist ship. He had to admit that despite the situation, he liked the feel of her in his arms, the smooth contact of skin against skin. In fact, he liked it enough that she'd be noticing if he didn't move soon. That was one thing the males of his kind shared with the human males, obvious sexual interest and arousal. She didn't need that. She needed his strength, his compassion, and she would have it as they found the truth together.

He could feel her conflict, her attraction to him warring with the terror of the recent past. *She needs more than sex, she needs tenderness and emotional connection after her captivity.* He knew what she needed, and despite the fact that it was his duty to find the truth and deal with it, the urge to be the one to connect with her, for whatever reason, and to comfort her tempted him.

Chapter 3

"**M**ove," Sue growled at the alien. They'd stretched out together like bunkmates, his body weight pressing her to the couch. *Damn, he's built.* A quiver of motion shuddered up her back as anxiety flooded her body. He was exactly the body type she preferred, but even for her he was moving along a little fast. She lashed out, shoving at his chest.

"You need to let me touch you," he breathed in her ear, his hot breath sending electricity straight to her nipples. "We need contact to have *m'iitar*."

She pushed him aside enough to slide off the couch. Her ass hit the floor but only for a second as she scooted away from him. "We aren't having anything!" she snarled. "Certainly not some sort of kinky alien sex."

He grinned, a slow sly of grin of pure arrogance that males of his sort, anywhere, had perfected over the millennia.

She stood, stiffened her back and narrowed her eyes at him. "I won't be pressured. This is sexual abuse. I'll demand a new investigator."

That stopped the smile.

"You will not. I am your Examinator. I regret that your

impression of our contact is disturbing, but it is also incorrect. *M'ütar* is the mind contact we have begun to share." The grin came back as if he somehow knew some small part of her found the idea tempting. "Not something…kinky."

She turned her back on him, wrapping her arms around her naked chest, and huffed a breath between her lips. Confusion warred with desire inside her. For a second she'd felt attracted to Kiis. Now she wanted him far from her. He had the powerful sort of physique that she'd always gone for, but how could she want a man when she didn't even know his first name? And an alien, for god's sake, let alone her potential prosecutor. Not that something like that would have stopped her before. If she'd wanted something she'd have gone for it.

For the first time in her sexual adulthood she waivered, and the hesitation made her doubt herself even more. The conflicting emotions were strong enough to make her want to lash out at his smug face, even as she realized that she'd felt safer in his arms than she had in months.

"Touching makes the contact possible between our races. The more we touch, the deeper the contact will be. The more certain I will be of the truth. Among my people it is accepted for *m'ittar* to lead to intimacy as the contact deepens, but it doesn't have to result in anything more than an embrace if you choose."

"You just surprised me. That's all." Her voice once again let her down, and she hated how much it gave away, how shaky she sounded. *When did I become such an earthbound wuss?* she berated herself. *Be a marine, woman.*

"I am sorry if this surprised you, but I must know what happened."

She turned to face him, her confusion shifting into anger. He was standing now too, and much closer than she had thought. "What happened? What happened was I was kidnapped, held hostage, tortured and nearly killed." Her voice wavered and rose in pitch as she continued. "Yes, I did give them information. But I had to give them something or they would have killed me. I gave them as little as possible—just enough that they were sure to be destroyed!"

"Hush, be calm. I understand your pain. Let me help you through this." He reached for her, pulled her to him.

His arms surrounded her, a gentle embrace offering warmth and support. Never in her life had she wanted that from a man, needed it. She was a military career woman. Why would she ever need anyone to smother her this way? But she leaned into him, accepted his touch and closed her eyes to the past.

HE KNEW she was in pain. Her bones and skin had been healed, but she hurt, deep inside her psyche. He couldn't stand it, couldn't let the pain continue, whether she was guilty or innocent. He pulled her body to his, feeling her taut muscles trembling with fear and confusion, even hatred—directed at him or at those who had tortured her, or possibly even at herself. He wasn't sure. And that was the point—he needed to be sure.. But the pain needed to stop or he, too, would fall into it.

He held her close, feeling her cool skin against his. This species' body temperature ran lower than his, reminding him of the blue-skinned race he'd counseled last year. They hadn't made it into the Confederacy. Their government had been unable to accept the treaty conditions, and the people as a whole were territorial and ingrained with a superiority complex that made contact with multiple species nearly impossible without aggression. It had been a terrible loss—for them, for the Confederacy and for Asler's career. But it wasn't a choice he regretted.

The humans, though, were different. There were hot emotions under their cool skin. And not all areas of their skin were cool. He could feel the hot points of her hardened nipples even through his *chammiss* robes. Her eyes, too, seemed to pierce him with heat.

She was biting her lower lip. If she'd been Inarrii he would have comforted her by drawing her into a kiss, a taste of her silken lips. He would stroke her mind and body until she could relax enough to be calm. But she was human, and he could feel her confusion and fear in a complex tangle of emotions. That she seemed to have a hint of interest in him must be ignored in the face of what they would have to go through together to attain the truth. So instead he opened his mind to hers, took her to a place he knew and loved.

Red haze drifted around their bodies as they stood entwined on the black sands of his home. Clear water lapped at their feet, but it was mostly obscured by the red morning fog.

She pulled away from him with a gasp, her eyes no longer angry, but open wide with shock. He held tightly to her arm to keep the contact open, smiling when delight filtered out the surprise.

"Where are we?" Her mental contact seemed as soft as a whisper to his senses.

"My home, or part of it."

Her eyebrows rose to meet the short bangs of her hair. *"An alien world. I've wanted to see one all my life."* Her eyes scanned the waters, the red fog, and the black sand. *"Is it always like this? What is this red stuff? And you have two moons..."* Her voice trailed off, then her shoulders drooped. *"I'll never really see this. They'll take away my space privileges, tie me to some land desk, even if I am found innocent."*

This fear he could not dismiss. He knew she believed it was true, and that perhaps her culture would require it. Unlike his people, they could never know what she truly believed had happened, only what they were told.

"That may be. But we have to reveal the truth, Susan, all of it." He slipped into the use of her primary name; titles were meaningless mind to mind.

"I don't know if I can—I don't know if I can do it, see it all again." She lowered her eyes. *"I don't want to. They hurt me in too many ways to talk about. They beat me badly, and—"*

He stopped her. *"Trust me. There will be no pain."* He raised her chin. *"We cannot stand to see pain in others. Inarrii must protect, heal."* He stroked her cheek. Her emotions assured him that she spoke the truth, that she feared experiencing the pain again.

She shivered, and a slight hint of the woman trapped inside the victim peeked out of the solemn expression in her eyes.

"Walk with me." He slid his hand down her arm to clasp her hand. *"Let me show you part of my world. There is time."*

They stepped closer to the water until her feet touched the clear waves and fingers of reddish mist grazed the edge of her *pettan*. *"It's so warm,"* she murmured.

"Most of my world is water, dotted with thousands of islands like this one. My home is only a few ridges away. I come here when I need peace."

They walked for a moment; she studied the landscape, and he watched her.

"It is peaceful. The sand is so soft. I've never seen black sand, but I know there is some on Earth, near volcanoes."

He pulled her to a stop and knelt, drawing her down to the sand. She hesitated slightly but then sat near him, following his lead as he ran his hand over the smooth grains and reached out to grab a fistful of sand, trickling the particles through her fingers.

"Inarrii are a sensual people. We prefer to touch, even embrace our surroundings. Everything on Inarr feels good." He squeezed her hand with his, but wasn't surprised when she quickly let go.

She looked up into the sky. *"There are no birds?"*

"No. Birds are something I believe are only on your world. I have never seen any. Would you show me one?" Casually he reached over to run his other hand along the skin of her arm. She started slightly but this time didn't pull away. Something

within him relaxed, the tightness uncoiling as he realized she was accepting him much quicker than he'd expected. The incredible gift of *m'ittar* had blessed them again. By bringing her to a place of his personal peace, he'd fulfilled her desire to see an alien world and had reached her in a way no other action could have. The gods blessed his mission.

He studied her has she scanned the horizon. Her smooth skin, naked of Inarrii *L'inar,* was intensely appealing. He swallowed as he realized that his need to comfort her was gone, satisfied as she relaxed and put aside her pain, but his desire for her was steadily increasing. The mission might be blessed, but that didn't mean it would be easy. He must put aside his sensuality and concentrate on finding the truth.

It was clear that her vulnerability, so appealing to his protective nature, was caused by her recent captivity. He'd read Agent Alinna Gaerrii's reports carefully as she'd met Captain Branscombe and they had indicated a strong, independent personality not given to hesitation or timid behavior. The change pointed to innocence, unless she had somehow fooled the Inarrii Agent. However unlikely that might seem, it was still something to watch for, especially considering how easily she was adapting to *m'ittar*. Her mind was very strong, and she was learning fast. Intelligence, beauty, vulnerability—no, the mission wouldn't be easy.

"How can I show you?"

He shook his head, her words confused for a moment with his more immediate desire. Clamping down on his response, he thanks the gods he'd left his *chammiss* robes on or she might have noticed the slight thickening of his *L'inar* as he responded to her in a way she would surely feel inappropriate. He *must* retain control over his attraction. He had a duty to perform and even if his initial assessment told him she was innocent, he must find the proof and be absolutely certain. Everything hinged upon that.

"Remember a bird, one you observed on your home world. That's what this is, a memory. I am not imagining this place, I am remembering it and sharing that memory with you. Just remember a time when you saw a bird in flight, and I will guide you in sharing that moment."

She hesitated, then closed her eyes. It wasn't necessary for her to close them, but he wasn't about to interrupt her when she was trusting him, trying something new. A bird would surely have innocent associations for her and relax her further.

"When I was young I would hike with a friend out of the city. We would stay out, sometimes overnight. When you get far enough away from the buildings there are more animals than just the usual city pests. There are seagulls."

Asler sucked in a breath as the terrain changed around them. He didn't have to help her. As Agent Gaerrii had reported, human *m'ittar* was stronger than anyone might have anticipated. From the beautiful coastal shoreline of his home, their surroundings morphed into a scrubby wasteland, tainted with the hint of city pollution. There were patches of green—long grass and thorny bushes. It wasn't what he had expected. Susan must have grown up in one of the heavily overpopulated inner continent cities. This patch of empty land would be all there was before another city began.

"You call them seagulls, but you are far from the sea?"

"They used to live mostly near the sea. Now they're everywhere and can survive by feeding on almost anything. They survived when even the vultures died. They're scavengers, but still beautiful, in their way."

A slight breeze brushed Asler's face, and he looked up to see a large bird, white and gray with yellow feet and a strong beak; its wings pumped the air as it maneuvered to land not far from him. He found himself shifting uncomfortably under the creature's beady gaze. Perhaps it would eat *him* if the chance arose.

"There were bluejays too." Her mental voice reflected a

34

hidden amusement at his reaction. The seagull faded away, replaced by a smaller bright blue bird with feathers tipped in white and black. It let out a little shriek and flitted away, leaving behind a light blue feather which drifted softly to the ground.

Alser reached down and picked it up.

"I'd forgotten about the feather. I kept it for a long time." She looked at it and then at their clasped hands. *"Is all of this really happening?"*

"The birds, this place—they are memories. What happens between us when we talk, that is really happening right now."

"It's like a dream. Or like the last two months were a dream." Despair laced her mental voice. *"A nightmare."*

Asler pulled her close. The embrace, intended only for a moment's comfort, seemed to be what she had been waiting for. Tears pooled in her eyes and spilled over her cheeks in fat droplets. The urge to comfort was overwhelming, enough that he could not stop the way his hand began to stroke her back, caressing *L'inar* she didn't have, or halt the kiss that moved his lips over hers in a gentle possession.

"Wait…" Her despair scattered by the surprise of his actions, Susan began to pull away. The beautiful flush of her skin reminded him that humans didn't expect these actions from a superior, or require them for comfort.

"I apologize. Inarrii comfort each other this way. I forgot for a moment you were not…"

"Not Inarrii." Her body did not stiffen with alarm as Asler expected. She actually relaxed, responding to either his kiss or his words just as a troubled Inarrii would. Now he was the one confused, but also relieved as he acknowledged to himself that he might have made a serious blunder with her case if that had not been her reaction.

Perhaps, for her, sensuality could be a key to trust and a deeper contact, just as it would with an Inarrii. With that thought he brought them back to the black sands of his homeworld.

"You are very tense. I would ask you to relax, but I know that

words are never enough. Allow me to deepen our m'ittar. I can only do this through contact."

She looked him the eyes, her glance seeming to measure him. Her gaze seemed to catch on the feather he'd pulled from her memory and brought along with them to his homeworld, its edge flaring out from the narrow pocket of his robe. Finally she nodded.

"Roll on to your back."

She lay back in the sand, stretching out her lanky body with a grace any warrior would be proud of. She rolled over, giving him her back and her trust. He lowered himself to the sand beside her and pictured the vial of oils he'd left at home, bringing one memory into the other and blending them as only a master Examiner had the ability to do. Unstopping the bottle, he breathed the scent in, a blend of herbs infused in *siland* oils that brought peace to a restless mind. A few drops on his hands and he began, slowly stroking her unmarked skin. He kneaded her muscles, applying pressure as he'd been taught by his first lover.

He ran his palms over the lean length of her back. The edge of her *pettan* had slipped, and he could see the dimples at the top of her tailbone. He swallowed hard. This contact, pushing the limits of her trust to deepen the strength of their *m'ittar,* also pushed the limits of his desire. He shouldn't have put off engaging in sex with the eager young officers on the ship. The urge to run his fingertips under the soft material of her *pettan* and pull it down to expose the rounded cheeks of her ass tightened his groin. When he realized that she was moving under his hands, leaning into the pressure of his palms, he nearly groaned aloud.

After a few moments she glanced back at him. Her eyes were solemn, and his heart stirred as he realized that despite his efforts, she could not imagine herself as anywhere other than still deep in trouble—her future, perhaps even her life in jeopardy. Sensual she might be, but her mind moved in complex patterns.

He took a chance, lowered his mouth again to hers. In the contact of *m'ittar*, desire became reality. Their lips touched, his questioning, hers answering. He parted her mouth with his tongue, tasted her as he'd wanted to since she'd been healed.

She rolled to one side. Her arms returned his embrace, stroked his back. The soft lines of his *L'inar* markings across his torso stiffened into ridges as she stroked him, unknowing what her actions were suggesting to him. He groaned with desire as her hands explored, but released her when she broke the embrace.

HIS KISS, so gentle, and so sensual was a marvelous distraction. He didn't pressure her. For a few minutes she forgot where she was, and why she was there. More importantly she forgot what had happened before, or at least she could pretend to forget. There was something in his intense green eyes, something…honest. *He's delicious.* Admitting to herself that she wanted him was easy enough in this unreal alien place. *He's…beautiful.*

Sue stood and faced the lapping waves of black water. She heard the soft rustle of sand as he stood as well and imagined the way his eyes would be watching her. Would they be filled with pity?

All her adult life had been spent in the military. She'd fought for every advancement and never shown a moment's hesitation to stand up for herself or her brothers in arms. She was tough, never needing all the mushy emotional crap she saw in the vids. It wasn't for her. If she wanted a man, she took him or let him take her, but never worried about intimacy. And if that was sometimes a lonely existence, well, that was what life had in store for her. Sex was sex.

But sex with this man, this alien, wasn't going to be

that easy. She could feel it. He was nearly the opposite of every man she'd ever been with, the way he seemed to consider every action, never jumping right in like she would have. If she followed her hormones this time, it would be complicated.

"Between Inarrii, sensuality is an experience that offers comfort. Forgive me if I have taken this too far." His mental voice rumbled with what she thought might be restrained passion but also carried the weight of complete sincerity. She turned back to him. There was no pity in his expression. He honestly wanted to soothe her, make her relax enough to find the strength to face the past.

She made a choice, and stepped in to kiss him again. She'd never shared more than the hot sweaty motions of sex, but this time she wanted more. He was offering her a tenderness that seemed to chase away the dark, that made her remember herself as her body pushed for more. The more she desired him, the more she felt like herself.

He hesitated. Was her kiss was tainted with her desperation to forget? Or perhaps he sensed the culmination of a lifetime of loneliness. But as she ran her hands over his forearms, he shuddered and met her lips again.

The preliminary reports on the Inarrii, and her former superior's comments were correct. The markings over most of Kiis's body were not tattoos, they were something else. The more she touched them, the firmer they got, forming ridges that rose above his skin. In some places only a few millimeters, and in others nearly an inch.

She ran her fingers over the ridges and looked up in time to see his eyes dilate. He liked it—no, she was pretty sure he *loved* it. She stepped deeper into the embrace, reached around him to stroke the ridges on his neck. She slid her hands under the edge of his robes, traced the lines as they curved down his back. They seemed to cover him, and she grinned as she wondered just how far they went. *Hell. If I wanted someone before, I just took them, right?* She pushed herself further. *I'll find out just how far they go, have a little fun, and all this shit will be over before I know it.* She liked sex, enjoyed it as often as she could. So why stop now? *My career is likely over anyway, and this isn't even my real body, for fuck's sake. I want him, want to imagine something more than a quick lay.*

I want more.

Groaning, he pulled her down with him onto the fine black sand. For an instant she wondered if he had read her mind, knew her intention to take whatever pleasure she could and to hell with the consequences. Or worse, did he realize she wished for something she couldn't hope for, emotional attachment? The red fog had nearly dissolved, and a yellow sun, so like her own, now bathed them in mild warmth. He laid her back, covering her with his hot skin. His lips raced across her earlobe, cheek and mouth to devour her. Her questions evaporated with the intensity of his touch.

Hunger. That's what she sensed from him, but not anger. She remembered that feeling all too well. Suddenly his weight seemed crushing, and she fought to breathe.

It flashed back to her. The pain she'd endured in captivity. Her mind bucked.

"*No!*" She gasped and pushed at the man covering her. Blackness crouched on the edges of her vision. She *would not* be sucked back into that memory, not now.

"*Susan, look at me. That is the past. I am here now. You are safe.*" Kiis held her, soothed her.

"*He...hurt me.*"

"*I know, but that is not now. That is the past. It's gone, Susan. Trust me.*"

"*I...I don't even know your first name,*" she stuttered. Somehow, the waves of panic the flashback had caused were fading. The weight of Kiis's body no longer seemed constricting. Heat radiated from him. Even though she was desperate for his touch, to feel connected in a way only he could make her experience, maybe rushing into sex and intimacy wasn't such a great idea. She looked into his eyes. "*Don't look at it. Don't look at that memory.*"

"*Shhh.*" He touched her short cropped hair. The warmth in his eyes, the caring, nearly eclipsed the desire she saw in their depths. The combination shook her, made her swallow as she realized how intensely he was focused on her. *"I am called Asler. Be here with me now, in the present. Just be with me."*

Chapter 4

A sler slipped from her mind, pulled the two of them back to the reality of the ship. He led her psyche into a deep sleep before releasing her entirely. His senses still reeled drunkenly as he lay with her on the bench in his office. Who could have imagined that the cool-skinned humans held so much passion and heat? He'd nearly given in to his desires and taken her as he would have any Inarrii woman, case be damned.

He drew a shaky breath and thanked the gods things hadn't progressed further. Where was his Examiner control? What he needed to do with this woman was find the truth. To do that, he couldn't treat her as he would an Inarrii, no matter what his instincts were telling him she needed—or even openly *asked* for.

The contact between them, the *m'ittar*, had been inex- orably strengthened. He would be able to take her through her past without her rejecting him, without her being able to stop the flow of images. He shut his eyes against the innocence on her face as she lay beneath him. She had shied violently away from the thought of her torture. She would feel betrayed if he forced her through it, forced her to remember it all only so he could decide if she had been party to the terrorist attack in any way, or if she were as guiltless as her sleeping face appeared. The urge to protect her from this pain pulsed within him. She was so different from other women and the way they made him feel.

Perhaps he shouldn't have taken things to such a physical level so quickly. But in *m'ittar* there was no way to lie—they had both wanted the sensual contact almost immediately, and in Inarrii culture, this contact was perfectly acceptable. In the face of her recent painful experience he desired, more than anything, to heal her wounds and comfort her. Sex shouldn't have been part of the equation, and yet it seemed that it was already part of the way they reacted to each other.

Asler slid from her embrace and rose above her. He wouldn't need sleep for some time, but humans needed to rest about every ten hours, if possible. Inarrii had much longer cycles, going twenty-five to thirty Earth hours before needing a sleep period. The ship had no hour-based schedule.

He looked down at Susan, admired her beautiful skin. A flick of his hand over the side of the couch turned its air blanket on to a warm setting.

Susan's skin still flushed with a ruddy color across her cheeks and down her neck and breasts. Passion. Surprisingly she had been able to feel it with him, had reached for it in his arms even after the torture she'd experienced. There was no question that she had been hurt badly by the terrorists. The question was, had the torture happened before or after she told them the location of the Confederacy ship? And how much had she told them? Were there more terrorists than the few found and killed onboard the attacking ship? They needed the answers, and needed them soon.

What the Confederacy hadn't told the humans was just how close the alien Ravagers were to Earth. They would soon lay waste to the fragile planet if no Treaty had been established. Even with one in place, the Ravagers would likely attempt to loot and destroy anything left unguarded on Earth.

He ran a light touch over Susan's short hair. He liked these humans. In particular, he liked this one very much. Being within her mind allowed for an understanding of her psyche that would take years without *m'ittar*. She was a strong individual with depths that begged to be explored. Their planet should not be left unprotected, to be ruined. His feelings were not only based on the obvious advantages Earth's resources would bring the Confederacy. His inner sense told him these people would be very important to his own, and that this woman would be important to him.

Since the full development of his *m'ittar*, he'd focused everything on his career. His clan relied on the younger men and women to bring them honor. That honor became a kind of currency on Inarr and within the Confederacy, where Inarrii were present. He'd never taken the time to look for a mate, although he'd always imagined it might happen some day.

He shook his head at the direction his thoughts were taking. Nothing was possible until the truth had been established and dealt with.

Quietly, Asler made his way to the cleansing unit. Spending time in the ultrasonic cleanser could be very relaxing if it was put on the lowest setting. Susan would sleep for at least four hours if he understood the human physiology he had studied. He'd take a break in the cleanser and then file his report.

As he stood inside the unit, he waited for peace to consume him again, to restore his equilibrium. It didn't come. She wouldn't leave his thoughts. He left the cleanser and skirted the office to enter his private bed chamber. In silence, he logged his time with Susan in his private records. An Examiner kept detailed reports, secure both physically and legally. What happened in any interrogation was private to all but the Examiner, at least until it was time to present any findings.

Upon returning to the office, his eyes were drawn to her relaxed body sprawled guilelessly across the couch. He moved to stand over her. Would these hours ever end? Despite his training to uncover the truth, there was something more that compelled him to be with her. Something surprising. He wanted to be with her, wanted more from her.

Asler sighed and stepped away, paced the short room twice as he tried to grasp the underlying current of the surprising desire. The woman wasn't even Inarrii. Perhaps he really had been too long without the comfort of his kind. Without sexual release. His eyes trailed over Susan's sleeping form again. He turned to make a third silent pass through the room when his communications desk beeped.

He strode to his desk, grateful not to have to question himself again. The communication panel slipped open to his touch, extending the seat and flashing the visual panel open to show him the Confederacy logo from the Inarrii outbase that had been secretly established on one of Jupiter's minor moons. Very few of the humans were yet aware of its presence, but they would be grateful of it if the Treaty was passed in time to protect them from the approaching Ravagers.

He signaled his acceptance of the communication to the desk and watched with unease as the face of one of his Inarrii commanders and old friend, Jannii Finar, filled the screen. Lines of stress radiated across the man's face.

"*Inar tel sahür—*" Asler began the formal greeting to his superior, but the Inarrii cut him short with a wave of his hand.

"Examiner Kiis, do you have the human Starforce Captain Branscombe?" Jannii asked intently, his voice taut with tension. The words were automatically translated to the human standard by the computer, Asler having programmed constant translation to aid in his fluency.

"Yes, she has been physically healed, and we have

begun the process of deep *m'ittar* connection. What is wrong?"

"Is there any problem with your bond, since she is human? Will you be able to find the truth?" Jannii pushed. "Will you be able to discover exactly what she told the terrorists?"

Asler stared at the screen. Something was seriously wrong. "What happened?"

"There's been another attack. This time they hit our outbase on the Jupiter moon. It was well planned, Kiis. There were two deaths, both Inarrii, and more damage than we expected. Hydroponics were affected, communications partially shut down." His eyes bore into Asler's. "There was more damage than we would expect from human weaponry. And they shouldn't even know we are here. Only the mobility of the small fighters saved us."

Asler's heart thudded. His commander's implication was clear. Some other race could be involved. It was possible an unknown entity had powered the attack under the guise of human anti-alien terrorism, someone strong enough to be a real threat to them all. The Ravagers could be here, although this kind of calculated subterfuge wasn't their usual style.

That the small fighters had aided the base was of special importance, as they had been provided by the human Starforce Marines, guided by the very officer who had made first contact with the Inarrii. This aide would allow the Treaty negotiations to continue, despite the taint of any human anti-alien dissident group.

"There will be no difficulty. When we touch, *m'ittar* is possible. I took her under, mind to mind. Our bodies are... similar." Asler shifted uncomfortably as his ridges hardened under his *chammiss* robes. He hoped in vain that they didn't show above the neckline. "The more we touch physically and mentally, the easier contact becomes."

Tension drew away from his commander's face,

although it remained in his eyes. "I wish I could hear more about it. Your *L'inar* are rising."

Asler cleared his throat. So much for the hope that Jannii wouldn't notice. Memories of Susan's body against his pushed at him, hard. "It will work."

"You have to get answers, Kiis. We need to know her involvement and what she told them. We need to know who they are. I know this attraction will not pull you from the truth." Jannii was once again the commander, and his tension was back. Asler felt as though he'd been shaken.

With a short salute and a formal well-wishing, they signed off.

Asler leaned back in the communication seat. It shifted with him, the low back rising to cradle him as he ran through the short communication again in his mind. His instinct told him to trust Susan Branscombe, and it wasn't because of the kisses they had shared. But could he believe in himself when he had such an immediate response to her? Not so much physically—his race were highly sensual and it was expected that that could happen—but emotionally? Could he trust that he would find out all that she knew, even subconsciously, when he felt such a connection and desire to protect her?

He also sensed that she had certain doubts and even a feeling of guilt over what had happened. Could she be, even unwittingly, marginally responsible?

A soft rustle behind him alerted Asler. He turned and met Susan's eyes. It was impossible to think of her as Captain Branscombe now. How long had she been awake? How much had she heard?

"So, will you discuss how good I was with him later? After you make me relive the pain? After you lock me up? That appears to be the plan—you screw me in my mind before you screw up my life permanently."

He looked away from her eyes, eyes so alert, so condemning, even when her body still wore the sleepy flush of fulfillment.

Chapter 5

Sue looked away after lashing out at Asler. Hurt had poured from his eyes when she accused him of planning to use her, and she couldn't handle that, not right now. Not when she already knew that she was wrong and hated herself for it. The words had just poured out, full of hatred. She was disgusted with herself. The man was only trying to do his job, and no matter how he had come across it, was she who had crossed the line first.

Still, how could he feel hurt when it was her future at risk?

She sat and pulled her knees up, hiding her breasts. A flush ran across her cheeks as she thought about what they had experienced together, mind to mind. She felt more naked than she had before. She'd almost had sex with the man who was either going to defend her or lock her up.

The couch vibrated softly under her, its heat a soothing comfort now that the warmth of Asler's body had faded from her skin. She wrapped her arms around her knees and lowered her head. "On Earth, we have a saying: 'Don't kiss and tell'."

"I'm sorry. While I would never discuss the details of anything intimate between us, my commander must be kept informed of the process of our *m'ittar* and the investigation."

"I'd like to go to my room," she muttered.

He sighed. "Again, I must apologize, Susan. You will have to stay with me for the duration of the investigation."

She jerked her head up at that, staring at him. "What? I have to be with you every minute? I get no privacy at all?"

"This is the condition of your investigation. You are under…house arrest, I believe would be your term. It is either stay with me, or be held in restraints in the hold."

She glared at him. It maddened her further that he simply stared back at her. She was half tempted to take him up on it, to go to jail until the damn trial was held. *Who the hell does he think he is?*

"Do not imagine that you would be happy in such a place, Susan," he said. "You would not. Also, you should consider that to place yourself in those conditions is to take on the appearance of guilt, even if you are not guilty. Appearing in restraints before any hearing would not lend to your credibility."

She stood, anger driving her to momentarily forget how naked she'd felt an instant earlier. "Quit reading my mind. This is crazy. I am not guilty. I didn't tell them a damn thing that was really helpful. I just made sure that those bloody terrorists would end up being blown straight to hell."

She strode around the room. There wasn't even a pillow to kick. She huffed and crossed her arms. "How long?" she demanded. "How bloody long will this take?"

He leaned back in his chair, his eyelids half-shuttering those fabulously bright green eyes. A small smile lurked at the corners of his mouth. "You didn't seem in such a hurry a few hours ago."

"Never mind that. I was simply carried away in the moment. It's these damn mind games of yours. The exotic backdrop." *The incredible heat and feel of your lips,* she admitted to herself. "You have no right to treat me like this."

The smile faded. "I told you. We need to find out the truth. The *m'iitar* will allow me to be absolutely certain of your involvement." He hesitated for a moment then continued. "We can try to stop the sexual element of the contact if you require it. Doing so will be difficult, as there is no way to lie in *m'ittar* and it is a sensual connection by its very nature, but it can be done."

He turned and gestured at the communication screen behind him. "I believe you heard my commander. There has been another attack. Two of my people have been killed." He stood and gripped her arm, looking deep into her eyes. "You may know something that may help, even if you are not aware of it. Everything is locked in here." He touched her temple gently, the warmth of his fingertips lingering after even such a brief caress. Instantly *m'ittar* joined their minds.

"What do you mean? I didn't tell them anything important, hell I didn't even know anything about a base—a secret base, and I might add that I seriously doubt any of my people are aware of one."

"You possibly saw or overheard something while you were being tortured. Or you could have been witness to others passing information, even if you did not pass it yourself." He tightened his grip on her arm; the heat from his hand seemed to brand her. No memory world took them away from the present. This was it, a moment of complete truth between them. *"You may have told them something you are not even aware of."*

She tried to wrench away from him, aware that doing so would pull their contact apart. The fact that she couldn't didn't surprise her. The reality was that she didn't truly want their contact to end—even when she knew the truth was about to be shockingly clear. *"I know exactly what I told them."* Tears sprang to her eyes. *"I told them what I had to, but not a bit more. Not enough for them to succeed, only enough to get them in trouble so they would fail. So they would die."* She lowered her head, staring blindly at the textured floor.

He laid his palm against the smooth skin of her back. *"And you would die, too."*

She shuddered, the tears falling down the curves of her cheeks. *"I was so tired, I didn't care anymore if I survived. I couldn't expect it...or hope for it."*

He pulled her into his arms. *"You're safe. And I know that you believe you are innocent. Now we must prove it, and we must discover everything that is buried in your subconscious."*

She turned in his arms to face him, to bury her face into the incredibly soft robes he wore with such grace. He held her, towering over her, his bulk dwarfing her long lean frame. For the first time in years she felt small, vulnerable. As a military woman she was expected to be rough, tough, and ready to fight. This feeling, of being cherished and protected, felt...alien, and yet, at this one moment, it was more than welcome. It was right. Perhaps it was *because* he was an alien that she could admit to her need for his care. He had no expectations from her other than the truth.

Sue rubbed her cheeks over the soft material stretched across his chest. She slid closer, moved into an embrace that welcomed intimacy. It felt natural, necessary. She looked up at him, into his earnest gaze and lifted her lips to meet his.

The air around them changed. He'd brought them back to his beach. His mouth lowered to hers, and she welcomed the sensation. Within their joined minds she began to realize anything was possible. With the transition into *m'ittar*, he'd shed his *chammiss* robes in favor of a light *pettan* like she wore, baring much of his skin to her touch. She ran her hands over his naked chest. He groaned with desire as she explored.

Each *L'inar* whorl of color rose into a light ridge as his desire mounted. They stretched across his scalp, down the back of his neck and shoulders, arms and torso, up his thighs and into the private areas shielded from her sight by the *pettan*.

"We aren't built quite the same as humans. Close, but not quite."

She traced the growing ridges of color on his chest with her fingertips. He shuddered. *"Tracing someone's L'inar is an invitation to sex and possibly to a serious commitment."*

"I want...I want you to treat me like an Inarrii, to comfort me like you would one of your people. I want..." She stopped as his lips met hers. He knew what she wanted.

Susan traced the lines curving down his back, followed them as they meandered beneath the loose *pettan*. She slid her fingers inside and cupped his ass. He kissed her again, slowly, his lips tracing hers in a tender path. In return she stroked the thin ridges of *L'inar* over his hipbones and was rewarded with feeling a level of satisfaction as they stiffened under her touch. She ran her blunt fingernails along their paths, drawing a deep moan from deep inside his chest.

"Stop," he groaned the word against her.

"Why? I know you like it." She slid her hands into the soft material of the *pettan*, following the lines along his hips.

He groaned and grabbed at her hands, stilling them. *"You are driving me crazy."* Hunger edged his mental voice.

"Good."

He kissed her harder and slipped his fingers into her *pettan*, neatly sliding the garment down her hips. *"Let me give you something else to think about."* He took her hand and lowered her down to the black sand beach. He kneeled back, crouching between her thighs. All thoughts of his ridges—his differences—slid away as he parted her. He lowered his head, his unbound hair caressing her thighs. His generous mouth nuzzled her, his warm breath teasing her until she whimpered for more.

Licking, then sucking, he explored her, found all the spots that made her body shudder under him. She ran her fingers through the long silken mass of his hair. Along his scalp she fingered the tiny ridges that ran under his hair and rubbed them as he brought her closer and closer to completion. She savored the moment, a surrender to a stranger whose alien body commanded hers in a way no one had since she had first entered the Starforce Marines, who made her forget everything but the moment. But as she climbed the final peak, she remembered that he wanted more from her than this moment; he wanted the truth.

With a moan Sue gave in, pushing away her doubts and shedding the final part of her that held back, toppling slowly over the edge into orgasm. She opened her eyes and arms to Asler, holding him as he stretched out in the black sand beside her.

"I want to taste you," she whispered to him. Despite the soft sound of the nearby waves, the quiet of the place seemed unnatural, increasing the intensity of the moment.

He hesitated, holding his body away from hers. He grimaced. Had she done something wrong?

"I'm sorry," she began.

"No, no." He lowered himself onto the black sand beside her, leaning on one elbow and reached with his other hand to caress her cheek. *"To follow the L'inar lines along the path of a man's saiin, especially with your lips or tongue, is to court a permanent mating—marriage."*

"Oh!"

He pressed against her, the dark ridges along his skin so hot against her. *So different,* she thought as she leaned into his embrace. But as she looked into his eyes and read the passion there, she understood that despite their differences they were in many ways the same.

She ran her fingers over him again, lightly stroking the ridges that ran along his abdomen. His emerald eyes darkened as she reached for his cock.

She murmured in appreciation and took him in her hand, feeling the heat of him, the size of him. Thin ridges decorated his length, firmed as she stroked him. His taste was a forbidden desire. Something that part of her yearned to savor, despite the consequences. Instead she lifted her lips to his and met them with a desperate kiss. This was a moment stolen in time. For now she didn't need to think about what she had suffered or what would happen to her in the future. She had only to forget the past and enjoy the moment, to live in it with a being that promised to love her body, and love it well.

His hands roamed over her skin, and she returned the favor, each of them exploring the other's differences. She wanted to touch, to taste, but she held herself back, using only her hands as she explored him. Nothing held him back—he delighted in suckling her breasts, taking each nipple deep into his mouth and pulling hard until the pressure had her groaning aloud, squirming beneath his hands.

Her groans turned to soft pleas when he dipped one hand between her thighs, stroking her core. With sudden inspiration she took his other hand and brought it to her lips. She kissed the pad of each fingertip and then as he began to press into her, exploring the wet folds of her pussy, she sucked his index finger into her mouth. He moaned aloud, the physical metaphor affecting him as she'd hoped. She sucked at his digit as she would have enjoyed sucking his cock and was rewarded when his eyes darkened even more and his breaths grew ragged. She arched against him, sucking, and breathed in the scent of his hot skin. Hints of alien spices infused with male musk teased her, made her mouth water. She dragged her teeth over him as he parted her and slid one finger deep into her.

"Yes!" she groaned out the encouragement. But he took too long, seemed barely to stroke her, until she could stand it no more.

Sue gripped his shoulder and flung one leg over his hips. With a twist and a thrust, she rolled with him and pressed his back into the beach beneath them. His long hair spread against the ground, the hue of his hair contrasting like gold against the fine black sand. She leaned forward and took his lips, determined to possess them, but fell back with a gasp as she realized his fingers were still pressed against her core.

He grinned at her and teased her, pulling her quickly to join him in a rhythm over which she had no control. She rode it, spread over him and open to his touch, unable to do anything but follow his lead as he took her again over a crest of desire and into orgasm.

Sue's juices dripped and she gasped for breath. He shifted her, lowering her until she could feel the heat of his cock against her. She spread her legs wider, straining to reach the hot skin stretched so tightly over his throbbing member. Slowly he lowered her onto him, allowing only one ridged section of his cock into her at a time.

She tightened over each ridge. Each textured crest enhanced and prolonged the sensation of penetration, that moment when she was first truly opened by her lover. Sue found her moans harmonizing with his soft grunts of passion. *"Oh...my...God."*

She clenched his biceps with her hands, hanging on as she rode him, at first slowly, then faster. The ridges rubbed inside her, informing her of nerve endings she'd had no idea she possessed. She rocked against him, delving deeper into the sensation. With each swivel of her hips she could feel the pattern of his *L'inar* rotating against the sensitive skin of her pussy lips. A soft noise drew her attention to his face, and it was her turn to grin as she watched the control leave his eyes. She began to rock in a figure eight over him, and the sensation took both their breaths away.

Asler rolled over, taking her with him. He drove into her as he rose up on his elbows. She couldn't think, couldn't stop herself as she touched him anywhere, everywhere. Her lips brushed the *L'inar* across his chest and she licked and sucked at his hard nipples. He shuddered, thrusting so deeply into her she felt split in two. He roared her name, and she felt the spurt of his climax, felt its heat and joined it to soar for the third time beneath him.

With a jerk, their *m'ittar* broke apart. Gasping, their breaths racing, they held on to each other in the suddenly harsh light of Asler's office. Her jaw dropped open in shock, as the realization that they were both still clothed, her hands fisted into the soft material of his robes, hit her. She stared into the depths of his startled eyes. Neither could look away, and when she pressed herself back into his arms he welcomed her, wrapping his arms around her.

For the first time in her life, she clung to a man.

A sudden, odd noise interrupted their embrace with a quick start. She flushed with embarrassment and cursed her fair skin once again as she realized the source of the noise came from her own belly. *Great. It's embarrassing to be so obviously embarrassed, and now my stomach is protesting like I haven't fed it in weeks. So much for a little real-life sex. I could use some more of that...comfort.*

He grinned. "We have growling bellies too, the same as humans." He let her go and walked to the desk. With no small amount of satisfaction she noted that he swayed slightly as he stepped away. After tapping a few keys, he turned back and took her hand. "You've just gone through a major healing. Your body needs to be cared for." He stroked the pad of his thumb over the back of her hand. "Come with me."

ASLER WATCHED the little human woman take in the scene before them. Perhaps it wasn't the best idea, exposing her to their cultural differences so quickly. A meal in his room might have been better.

Her eyes were open wide as she glanced around. Couples lay on low couches in various degrees of undress, enjoying their meals and each other in equal and obvious delight. Her tongue flicked out, and she wet her lips.

No, she wasn't shocked and dismayed. She was shocked and aroused, he realized with a grin.

This was more than he'd hoped for. Her desire opened channels between them that allowed him greater access to her thoughts, her emotions, and her memories. His smile faded. Discovering the truth about what happened was becoming more important all the time—a second attack meant greater risk to the Treaty, and to the human world, whether they knew it or not. Susan believed she had done the right thing but still felt guilty, and he would soon have to discover why.

"What the hell is this, a lunch orgy?" she asked, never taking her eyes off the scene before her.

"This is how we enjoy our meals. This is a *sterali*. The couch will mould to whatever shape you require and has attached tables that revolve around the seat, lowering or raising as you request. It's quite comfortable." He led her to the nearest empty couch, held her hand while she sat down.

"I think they're enjoying a hell of a lot more than their meal." Susan's attention still focused on a nearby couple. A woman lay naked on her back on the soft *sterali*, which had reacted by levering her hips up, opening her to her partner's caress. Their meal lay half devoured as the *Inarrii* male licked at the sticky sweet syrup he'd spread on her thighs.

Susan's breath came quickly as the man worked ever closer to his goal.

"Perhaps you would enjoy some of the same?" Asler teased her.

"What?" she glanced at him, alarm in her eyes. "In front of everyone?"

"I meant the noodle dish."

"Yeah, right. Sure you did." Susan glanced around the room again. "No one cares that it's so public? Do you eat every meal like this?"

Asler took a seat beside her. He waived a hand over the low table which rose and hovered near his elbow. "*Yessin* for two, *rothan*, and *saiithan*," he spoke to the air.

"What's that?" Susan eyed him, and he found her suspicious glance oddly endearing, and arousing. Introducing her to *Inarrii* custom and cuisine was going to be a lot of fun.

"We don't eat every meal like this, no. This is a casual way of reaffirming ties, exhibiting bonds to others to ensure no mistake is made over who is involved in a permanent relationship and who is out of bounds, you might say." He lifted his hand to her shoulder, stroked that incredibly smooth skin. Her exotic lack of *L'inar* encouraged him to touch, to taste. "No one cares that is it is public—that is the purpose. I've just ordered lunch, some food I think you will enjoy."

She looked around again and he admired the blush of color that spread across her cheeks as she watched the couple nearby shift into an apparently universally appealing sixty-nine position. The male's *L'inar* were fully raised, and the female sucked and licked at them with abandon as his face lay buried in the crevasse between her legs. Another couple wandered over, caressing each other as they candidly watched the mating couple.

Asler observed Susan's nipples harden at the sight. She needed to trust him the same way. Opening to him now, in a way that she would consider 'in public' would go a long way toward establishing that trust. And, he admitted to himself, he wanted to have her now, like this.

He frowned. The urgency of his desire was becoming worrisome. He should not have such a strong reaction. He dismissed it after a moment. It had been some time since he relieved his needs, surely that was all.

A young woman approached, bearing a tray with two plates of steaming noodles and utensils, a decanter of *rothan*, two glasses, and a small plate of long cylindrical cookies. She placed it on the table and moved onto the next couch.

Asler took up a fork and swirled the noodles up into a bite. She watched carefully and seemed about to copy him when the couch beneath them shuddered. Plates rattled on the suspended tables.

"What—" Susan began, but her question stopped as the floor beneath them bucked, and the lights flickered.

Alarm tones sounded. Asler jumped to his feet.

"We have to get back..." His voice was lost in the sudden roar of explosive force that ripped through the room.

One side of the dining room outer wall crushed forward in the deafening boom. Thick acrid smoke began to fill the air. Asler's heart constricted as he sensed as much as heard the pained screams nearby.

Alarm bells continued to sound. He grabbed for Susan's arm, intent on getting her out of the unstable area of the ship. He had to find out what had happened, if there had been a third attack. But most of all he needed to be certain she was safe.

That fear tore at him with greater force when he realized she was no longer beside him.

Through the smoke he searched the room for her, his mind open and searching for her now familiar pattern, despite the pain he felt mounting around him. He staggered forward toward the worst of the rubble, brushed past the injured but still mobile Inarrii who were retreating from the disaster. He joined those who were attempting to help the more seriously injured.

Asler rushed to help a young officer pull a fallen light fixture from the crushed leg of a trapped Inarrii, only realizing after he'd gripped the debris that the victim was one of the Inarrii couple Susan had been observing earlier. *"Have you seen the human?"* he asked the officer as they yanked on the twisted metal.

"She's over there, near the fire crew." The reply was harsh and abrupt, mind to mind as Asler realized that it was this Inarrii's lover they were rescuing.

Fire.

Horror surged through Asler. Fire onboard was the worst thing that could happen on a spaceship. He strained, pushed aside the last of the ruined fixture, and pressed a quick hand to the moaning man beneath, dropping him deep into unconsciousness until medical help arrived. He absently waived away the young officer's thanks and stepped over the heavier rubble to tug at the crushed couch pressing down on the unconscious man's side.

Where are the Medtechs? Asler worked to stop the flow of blood. His eyes scanned the room.

There. Susan was pressing a flat piece of *sterali* cushion against the last of the flames, beating the oxygen-stealing monster to death.

Covered in filth, she had moved first to address the thing that endangered them the most, the uncontained fire. The fire crew arrived quickly to the scene, but Asler wondered why the automated system hadn't kicked in first. The ship had to be badly damaged. He grimaced as he pulled off his outer robe, then used it to press against the injured man's wound.

"Examiner Kiis, thank you. We'll take care of him now." The soft mental command alerted Asler to the Medtech now standing beside him. He stood back, let the man closer.

"Has the ship been hit?" Asler asked, although he doubted the Medtech would have much information at this point.

"An attack alarm was sounded, but that's all I know." The Medtech turned his attention to the care of the ashen-faced man below them.

Asler glanced back toward the fire only to find Susan quickly approaching him.

"What the hell happened?" Susan's chest heaved as she fought to get the question out and catch her breath.

"Come with me. We'll find out. An attack here…it shouldn't be possible." Asler hated the fact that his voice sounded so uncertain, even to his own ears. An attack really *shouldn't* be possible. The ship was one of the most heavily defended in the Confederacy contingent that waited upon the signing of the Treaty.

His mind retraced recent events: first the ridiculously simple attack on the Inarrii warship at the Earth Starforce Base; then the surprisingly powerful attack on the secret

Confederacy Jupiter Moon Base; and now this...what was driving the attacks?

Asler grabbed Susan's arm and led her toward the exit. Most of the other diners, injured and shaken, had been taken to safety, and only the damage crews remained.

"Thank you for your help!" a heavily protected fire-crew member called out to Susan as she passed.

She nodded, moving with Asler, keeping pace with him.

Her actions had been heroic, Asler reflected as he stepped over another ruined couch. She'd moved instinctively into danger to help, despite the fact that she was on an alien vessel, facing charges. His gut feeling, as humans so quaintly phrased it, was that she was innocent, and her unselfish reaction to the enemy attack only supported his feeling. She hadn't tried to escape or even to simply remove herself from danger. Instead, she'd acted to protect an alien ship and its crew.

Some might say she acted only to protect herself. But Asler could almost taste her innocence, her guileless need to do the right thing, even at the risk of her safety. Now he had to prove it and make sure that he had every piece of information available. And that meant accessing her memories of the terrorists.

Chapter 6

"Damage has been confined to level five, and the attacking force has retreated," the ship's captain explained to Asler over the communication panel. "The ships involved were unmarked, but definitely not of human origin."

Asler glanced over at Susan, who listened from her perch on the low couch. She took another mouthful of her dinner, clearly enjoying the *yessin* noodles she'd missed tasting at the dining room before the explosion. He'd ordered them brought to her here in his office instead. The scent of the savory dish tickled his nose, reminding him how unsatisfactory the nutro bar he'd eaten had been, devoured in seconds during the captain's report.

Susan's *pettan* and skin still bore the sooty marks from the fire in the dining room. A shiver ran along his *L'inar* as he thought again of how she risked being badly injured when she attempted to put out the flames.

"Injuries?" Asler asked the captain.

"Three Inarrii have been seriously injured. No deaths, but it was a very close call."

"Where did the attackers come from? Who are they?"

"That's what we'd all like to know, Examiner." The captain's face sagged under the weight of his concern.

"We're not even certain that the same ones were involved in the other two attacks, or if they are related to the initial terrorist attack."

Asler rubbed a hand over the back of his neck. More questions. They needed the answers, soon. "Understood. Has any of this information been passed on to the Earth Consulate? Are they aware of the attacks or how little we know? Is the Treaty in jeopardy?"

"At this point, the command decision stands. We keep knowledge of the new attacks to ourselves. The Human Consulate still believe the first attack belongs entirely to the terrorist group Terran Purity. We've passed on nothing to the contrary, and the Treaty discussions are continuing. Examiner Salis Fiiten is attending. As usual the lawyers are pulling everything apart and rewriting the Treaty." A hint of the captain's strong character seeped back into his voice, tinting his tone with mild sarcastic humor.

"Good. We will continue to investigate, and leave the defense to you. I expect, and I believe you do too, that these attacks will continue—the timing, the locations, are all tied to the Treaty talks."

"Except for this last attack, I would have to agree. Why attack us here? The Treaty discussions and even the dignitaries and lawyers involved are housed either at the Earth Starforce Base or at the Confederacy Jupiter Moon Base. Nothing is going on here."

"Nothing except Captain Branscombe."

The two men stared grimly at each other. "Right. *Tel sahiir denay.*" The captain signed off, wishing him good hunting.

Now both his commander and his captain were personally relying on him to find some sort of answer through Susan's memories. The Treaty would depend on it. Asler glanced over at Susan again, only to find her dark blue eyes avoiding his gaze. Her meal sat unfinished in her lap, a bite balanced on her utensil. She needed to be ready for this, but he couldn't put it off much longer.

. . .

SUE SLOWLY TOOK one last bite of the noodles, delaying the time when she would have to look up at Asler and tell him she was ready to explore her memories. She could feel his eyes upon her after he'd said his goodbyes to the captain of the ship. It had to be done, but fear took away even the spicy taste of the foreign dish. She didn't want to remember. As it was, she'd almost run when the smell of smoke had hit her in the dining room. The burning scent was too close to the way her flesh had reeked as it burned under her torturer's hand.

Had it only been a week ago that she'd experienced that indescribable pain? And now, if she understood what Asler wanted from her, she would feel it again.

In the face of danger, she'd kept her calm, helped put out the flames in the dining room, despite the wave of fear drenched memory. But could she do this? Re-experience every moment of torture, so that they might find some questionable piece of evidence she didn't even know she possessed? She was innocent of collaboration; that was easy to prove. But he wanted to search every memory for something that might be there. Or might not.

"Susan..." His voice caught at her. She knew it was time, knew he wanted her to work with him now, to move through the past. She didn't want to disappoint him, she realized. She didn't want him to know she was a coward, that the thought of doing this terrified her. When had she come to care what this man thought?

"Susan, I know you are afraid." Asler stepped closer to her, lifted her chin to look into her eyes. "I'll tell you again —there will be no pain."

"No pain, but the memory of it."

"I'll be with you."

She pulled away from him. "I can't do it!"

He took a seat near her, careful not to touch her. "Your

people don't know everything. Your race is innocent of the danger that is out there. That is coming for you."

He had her attention now. She stared into his bright green eyes, a new fear gnawing at the edge of her consciousness.

"What danger?" Her voice rang sharply in the stillness of his rooms.

"I am not supposed to release this information, but I feel you should understand the real risks here. If we cannot resolve these attacks, determine their source, the Treaty is in danger. And if there is no Treaty, your planet and your people are in grave danger."

She sucked in a breath, clenched her fists as she stared at him. "What exactly do you mean?"

"There are forces outside the Confederacy that are waiting on an opportunity to step in and drain your planet of its resources. The Confederacy calls them the Ravagers. You might call them pirates. There is some evidence that points to the involvement of non-humans in at least two of the recent attacks. The Ravagers may already be in the area. They approach an unprotected planet—"

"We aren't unprotected," she interjected, Starforce pride stiffening her spine.

"Susan. These people are killers like you have never seen. They will destroy entire cities as examples, after forcing your people to surrender everything. And then they will kill or enslave everyone who is left. They will strip your metals and your water and leave what is left to slowly die. Earth will be a dry, lifeless husk. The Starforce is too new, too underpowered to form any kind of effective defense. Your fighters will die in space before they are aware they are under attack." He paused. "Unless the Confederacy is here to make a stand and protect your Earth, your people are lost."

The blood drained from her face as she listened to Asler's strained voice describing the death of all she knew and cared about.

"I…I need a minute," she stammered.

"Susan…" He reached for her but she evaded his touch and stepped away from the low couch.

"Let me get cleaned up, please. And then we will do this. We'll go through it all." She smiled grimly, feeling numb, as though all humor had leached from her soul. "I want to help. I have to."

PRIDE, compassion, and more than a little lust for the human woman before him warred within Asler, creating an emotion he had no name for and no control over. He took Susan's hand and led her to his private lavatory. It was a luxury on board that his rank called for, even if he rarely made use of it. This was the first time he had ever shared it with anyone, and he was secretly glad that he had the ability to offer Susan a touch of comfort and solace before she endured what she feared most.

Once again she exhibited a level of bravery that reminded Asler why he had chosen to stand for the human side of the Treaty as an Examiner advocate. These people could only add to the Confederacy.

"There are extra robes in the closet here." He pointed out the narrow enclosure, then gestured to the transparent cleansing unit. "We use ultrasonic wave purifiers. I think you will find the added massage frequencies relaxing. I've set the timer—all you need do is step inside the stall." Asler explained the other features of the cleanser to Susan.

Then, because he wanted to, and perhaps because she looked so small and lost, he wrapped her in his arms. He rocked her for a moment; her small frame clutched him in return. "We can do it, Susan."

"I know." She sighed and pulled away from him. She shed her dirty *pettan*, its light color smudged from her battle with the fire.

Asler swallowed hard when she bent to drop it on the floor, the ripe curves of her buttocks causing his mouth to suddenly water. He stepped hastily back, giving her privacy and time to collect her thoughts. He must accomplish his mission. What feelings he had on a personal level must come second, if that, to protecting the Treaty.

He stepped into the main room and stared at the blank outer wall. His room was near the inner bulwark of the ship, giving the wall a slight curve. If he planned to live here for any amount of time, he would coat the surface with a scene from home. Perhaps the very beach he had taken Susan to in his mind. *I must take her to the real place.*

Asler shook his head. His mind had wandered again into an area it should not go. The future would not likely hold much opportunity for Susan and himself to remain together. Instead, they would determine the cause of the attacks, and then each would return to their regular courses of duty. She to her Starforce Marines, and he to his role of Examiner, but for much more standard inquiries.

As Examiner he had to face the harsh realities, bring forward facts in situations where people might rather not face the truth. Now he knew he must also face the fact that he had begun to care for Susan…perhaps it had begun even before he set eyes upon her. Now his feelings had grown into more than care. It was more than her ability to handle the difficult situation or his need to protect, more than her physical beauty, her obvious strength. It was also her courage, and her passion. All these qualities made her important to him.

Now he understood that he didn't want to lose her, either to the truth if she had disclosed too much, or to her duty if she were found innocent and was required to return to service. He wanted more.

"I'M READY." Sue touched Asler's shoulder. The man seemed preoccupied with something, sitting staring at the blank wall as she slipped into the room.

She did feel ready. The ultrasonic cleanser had been

more refreshing than an old-fashioned water shower or the ionic air blowers on board her ship. She'd relaxed under the waves of the massage and felt more ready than she had since she'd awoken from her healing. That and a more concealing robe she'd found in the closet gave her a mild confidence boost. It was as soft as silk, but thick like wool. Though the fabric was short on her, at least it covered everything.

It was hard to believe that she'd been healed so completely or that she'd been onboard the alien ship for only a few days. So much had happened so quickly, especially her rapid bonding with Asler Kiis. He was an alien, for godsake. Yet she found she had no doubt that Asler would help her through the memories, that he would make it bearable.

As he turned to face her she was struck yet again by the immediate attraction she felt for him. His *L'inar* lines stood out—literally—in the most satisfying way. It was good to be able to see just how he reacted to her with as much attraction as she felt for him.

"Susan," he hesitated, his face serious despite the height of his ridges. "I've been thinking about the *m'iitar*. I would like to offer you an option. There is a way to take you out of the memory, for us to be able to examine what is happening without you experiencing the actual pain or sensations of remembering."

Sue's hear beat faster. *Thank God.* "That sounds pretty good to me. But would we lose any details? That is what you are looking for, right? Details I can't remember but that might be there?"

"Yes, you and I would see everything held in your memory as though we were watching a show. We might, depending on the level of contact we can achieve, be able to discuss what we see as we are observing it happen."

"Let's do it."

"Wait." He reached out and stroked the edge of her robe along one sleeve. One corner of his mouth twitched up in a small smile. "This is the top half of my *pet-horin* for sleeping in the cold. It looks much better on you." He shook his head and continued before she could speak. "There are risks to reviewing the memories this way."

"Pajamas," she murmured, watching the soft rounding of his lips. "What kind of risks do you mean?"

"By taking you from the memory you may not be able to experience it again."

She turned from him as a shudder rippled down her back. "That sounds pretty good to me. I don't want those memories ever again. They're like a nightmare you know will haunt you forever. Frankly, if I could lose them I would be glad."

"Look at me, Susan."

She turned back to him. His green eyes nearly glowed. Her mouth watered. His lips pursed as he prepared to tell her something important, but all she could think of was how she would like to kiss them, kiss *him*.

"By altering your memories and, in effect, removing them, we might get more detail as they will be unclouded by your pain, and we can discuss what we see. But this will mean that these memories will be unavailable as proof in your investigation and possible trial. It could hurt your chances of being found innocent of treason."

"Can't you testify on my behalf?"

"I am an Examiner, and Advocate for your people, and I have been one for my own as well. If I open my memories for review, those I have of previous cases might also be revealed, risking other people's careers and lives. Anyone examining my memories would be able to review them unchecked. I would have to resign my position."

Sue thought it through, biting on her lip in anxiety. "We need the truth to try and stop the attacks, or at least to keep the Treaty progressing. If I am found guilty I'll be locked up, but at least I would know I had saved my world from being sucked dry."

"You're very brave, Susan." Asler's warm hands

encompassed her own, chasing the chill creeping across her away. "Come with me. We'll relax and initiate *m'ittar* at a different level." Sue hesitated, so he continued. "It won't hurt. I will never hurt you."

Her heart kicked. She believed him. Together they would discover any evidence her memories held. But first, for a little while, she would allow her desire to lead the way, allow herself to believe it was only the two of them, that their combined worlds were not waiting on their discoveries.

He led her to the second door off his sitting room. As she had suspected, it led to his sleeping quarters, although they weren't quite what she expected. After the spartan design of the sitting room and bath, she expected the same here. Instead she was greeted with lush red color on nearly every surface, from the dark red walls to the thick rug underneath her feet. The bed encompassed nearly half the room, its covers strangely shiny in their speckled red and black tones.

She took a step forward, but Asler held her arm and bent to speak softly into her ear.

"*Inar tel sahan yowlenaii.*"

She looked up at him. "What does that mean?"

"It means…welcome, and also that I hope you will stay a very long time."

Chapter 7

Asler's *L'inar* crested down the length of his back, the sensation honing his anticipation. Susan's beauty paled beside her bravery, her pureness of character. There was no way he could believe she would do anything to jeopardize the safety of her world. What they found now would be hard for her to bear—watching herself crumble under torture—but would surely validate her innocence. The trick would be in proving that to Starforce and the Confederacy.

His initial thought to gain Susan's trust, possibly through sex, for the purpose of revealing the truth wasn't necessary. She had the courage to face the truth without him, now that she knew the situation. But now he found that he wanted to earn her trust, wanted to support her through the difficult times ahead, and not just while they were in *m'ittar*. He would be there for her while she battled through the trial for her career, and whatever the outcome.

Susan stared up at him, a look of wonder on her delicate face. His *L'inar* stiffened around his scalp and neck. Was she beginning to recognize what they might come to mean to each other? At this moment he could admit he didn't want their time together, no matter how difficult, to end.

For the first time, he speculated about the commitment between Inarrii agent Alinna Gaerrii and human Major David Brown. He'd been the one to explain to Brown about what it meant for an Inarrii to mate.

He stroked Susan's cheek, then lifted his arm to run his fingers through her short hair. It reminded him of the early sunlight on his homeworld. So bright, so beautiful. He pulled her to him, circling her with his other arm, running his hand down her back. She sighed, relaxing into him as his fingers searched her skin for the *L'inar* lines he knew weren't there. So soft and smooth, her skin felt erotically naked without the ridges of his kind. In Inarrii, females' *L'inar* would rise like a man's, although not as noticeably and their patterns were different. Some females' *L'inar* were tightly woven around the sensual areas of their body and nearly invisible until they began to mate or reacted in fear of some sort.

Susan shuddered under his exploring touch, her nipples hardening against his skin, a reaction to pleasure that both races shared. Asler moved to celebrate the similarities just as he enjoyed the differences. Palming a breast, he brought his lips to hers and kissed her deeply. Gently, tangled in their embrace, he led her to the edge of the great bed.

"Make love to me, before we go back into the memory," she whispered against his lips. She gripped his forearms. "In person, Asler, not in our minds."

Internally he rejoiced. *She feels it—feels the possibility of so much between us. There is time for this. I will make the time.*

He levered her back onto the bed. Its sensors reacted to their combined weight, spreading the pressure across its surface, holding them gently as it warmed and began to vibrate gently beneath them.

"Whoa!" Susan laughed in his arms. "A vibrating bed. Why am I not surprised?"

Asler's heart warmed to her laughter. She'd been through so much, and had so much yet to come, and still she could find an honest sense of joy. Along with courage, this was what the humans would bring to the Confederacy. Their Earth held many resources, but perhaps the people would be their most important asset.

"You are a joy, ya'lenali." He thought the words he wouldn't say aloud: she was a joy; she was in his heart. He could feel it, but he must not say it. There was a tone to her emotion that tasted of desperation. Perhaps it was residual fear, but he could not add to the pressure she must already be experiencing by pressing feelings upon her that she might not return.

"What?" Susan raised her eyebrows at him. "What did you say?"

Asler froze for a moment. Had he vocalized the thought? *No.* But she had heard him. He swallowed hard. Their *m'ittar* contact had been progressing very quickly. He hadn't actually initiated it, or even been physically touching her in the instant he'd thought the words. True, they'd had an immediate physical attraction and intense contact since he had met her. Was it only four days ago? And two of those she had spent healing. But perhaps there were more similarities between human and inarrii than had been expected.

Susan was staring at him now, seemingly disturbed by his odd reaction.

He moved to nuzzle her, rubbing his lips against her jaw and neck, nipping slightly at her skin. "Nothing. You taste so good. Let me taste all of you. I want to find out every parallel between us, every way our differences mesh. Tell me what you like."

"No. No games, no talking, no thoughts. Just us touching. I need you," she whispered.

She tangled her fingers into his hair, drawing him to her for a kiss. Her other hand roamed his body, stroking his *L'inar*, and driving him insane with sensation. She lay beneath him yet took charge of his body as though he were a novice to the act of love. When she pulled her legs up to wrap about his waist and began to rock against him, he gave in to her driving force. She needed him, so she would have him, all of him.

Reaching down, he stroked her with his fingers and found her ready for him. He levered himself with one arm, holding her hips, and matched his rhythm to hers, slowly pressing into her. He rocked into her core with a steady beat that both of them gasping. Still, she wouldn't slow, despite the way her body responded to the sensation of his *L'inar* as they rubbed inside her.

Although she flooded him with sensation, he wondered at her urgency. As strongly as she reacted to him, her actions, like the tone of her emotional being, resonated with desperation. It was one he thought he understood. Soon they would know the truth, and perhaps it would be more than she could bear.

Asler's heart ached, even as he groaned in pleasure.

She shuddered beneath him, and called his name. Her body clenched tight against him and he shut his eyes tight as he followed her into a deep well of pleasure. Drowning in it, he spilled inside her and whispered the words another Inarrii would take for the beginning of a sacred promise. Finally he opened his eyes to look at her again, to enjoy the sight of her naked in his bed. Instead he found them lying on the sandy shores of his home, her back pressed against its black sands.

"I love this place, your home." Susan murmured to him, contentment rich in her mental voice.

Asler breathed deeply as he dealt with the shock this little human had served to him. Even the air scented of the red fogs of home. *"How did you do it?"* he demanded.

"Do what?"

"How did you begin m'ittar? How did you bring me to my own memories?"

Surprised flashed across her face. *"I...I don't know. I*

thought you did this, brought us here again." She struggled beneath him, tried to push him away but her held close, letting his greater weight hold him in place.

"No. You did." He looked around. *"This is not where I brought you to before. It is nearby, but I can see my house from here, up on the hill."* He motioned with his chin, not releasing her.

She craned her neck, trying to see it as well.

"You couldn't have seen that before."

"So you did it then, not me. How could I take us to a place I haven't seen?" She demanded.

"Exactly. How could you?" Asler stared at her.

Her cheeks grew flushed under his scrutiny.

So beautiful, so complex. But does she have more m'ittar abilities than this? If she can manipulate my memories when I am a trained Examiner, can she influence my judgment?

SUE STARED into Asler's electric green eyes. She'd seen it —a flash of doubt. Despite the warmth of his body pressed against hers, a cold finger of fear wormed its way through her guts. *"What is it?"*

"You brought us here…"

"So you say." Her face flushed as the first currents of anger stirred her heart. *What was he accusing her of? He had promised to help her find the truth, and now he was looking at her like a snake that could poison him with a single bite.*

"What is a snake?"

"What are you talking about?""You said I looked like I thought you were a snake." He muttered as he eyed her. Uncertainty darkened his bright green eyes. He rolled off of her.

She felt the loss of his weight and heat as though it were a part of her being pulled away with his movements.

"I didn't say that…I thought it, though." She sat up, pulling her knees to her chest. *"What does this mean?"* She looked away from him and flicked black sand from her calves.

"It means you have more m'ittar abilities than I ever imagined. Our research indicated humans were unlikely to have any true psychic

abilities, but Major Brown has demonstrated the ability to achieve *m'ittar to a basic extent.*"

"*So? I don't understand. What is the problem?*" She watched as he rose from the sand and paced before her. Her anger faded as she observed him. He had no body shyness; he seemed completely unaware that he flaunted his beautiful body before her.

As the thought passed through her mind, he paused mid-stride and stared at her.

"*I'm beautiful?*" The corner of his mouth lifted.

Now she felt her face flush for a different reason. A true grin formed on his lips as she squirmed in embarrassment. *Good God, this is ridiculous. What am I, thirteen?*

He knelt before her. "*Oh, no, you are a woman, full grown and beautiful. And complicated.*" He took her hands in his. "*From the first moment, you have amazed me. You resisted my m'ittar when we first met. Then as we touched, our physical attraction let me in to your mind. But still you are strong enough to push me out if you want to. Then, despite the fact that we were not in m'ittar, you heard my thoughts. Now you have taken us to a memory you should not even know I have, to a place you have never seen. And here, our contact is so open, we are exchanging thoughts that are not truly directed at each other.*"

Stunned, she tried to follow what he was saying. He reached to stroke her face. "*I am telling you, Susan, that you have all the beginnings of true m'ittar. That with training, you could be as strong in your mind contact as I am. You could, perhaps, be trained as an Examiner for your people.*"

She looked away from him and drew a deep breath. Her thoughts raced. Was this even something that she wanted? The idea was too farfetched.

For a moment she watched the clear water lap against the black sands. Only the sound of the low waves and the light warm breeze reached her ears.

Finally she spoke. "*My people believe that I might be a traitor. Even if I can prove that isn't true, they will never accept me with some sort of super powers.*"

"*Let us deal with one problem at a time. We must find the truth, both for your trial and in hopes that it will give us some clue about the terrorists and defense against the Ravagers.*"

"*I want to start now, Asler. I shouldn't have put it off, asking for time with you like this.*" Sue stood, but as she began to brush the sand from the back of her thighs, Asler stopped her.

"*Like this, Susan.*" He slowly visualized *pettan* and the top from his *pet-horin* to cover her lightly.

"*Thanks.*" Suddenly she felt so tired. She'd only slept for a short nap since arriving on the ship. But there was no way she was going to put it off any longer. The memories needed to be explored. The treaty could not be held up, certainly not if she could help it.

"*We will begin in the morning. I can feel how tired you are. I cannot cause you harm, and I know how hard this is going to be.*" Asler raised his hand to stop her before she interrupted him. "*Tonight we will test the theory. In the morning we will begin the work. You did not stop the inquiry.*" He moved in and wrapped his arms about her, drawing her close to his chest. "*Our contact, our sex, it will all play a part in the level of m'ittar we can achieve. The deeper the level, the more likely we are to succeed in the m'ittar densah, the external memory.*" As he finished speaking an odd sensation slid through her and she realized they had stepped from his memory back into the red décor of his private chambers.

Sue pressed her face into the smooth skin of his chest, scenting the purely masculine aroma that was his alone. Her heart ached. She was tired and lonely, even in his arms. Did he mean that he was glad they had sex purely because it would help his work? That it would aid the treaty? Did he have any of the feelings she could feel forming in heart?

"Let's begin."

Chapter 8

Asler took Susan's hands. He could feel the tension in her, anxiety over witnessing her own past, her own pain—but not fear. Somehow, somewhere, she had come to trust him. His heart warmed to the thought. But he too, trusted her.

Despite the fact that she had unknown *m'ittar*, he had no trepidation about what they would do. Instead, he felt elated. They would explore her memories together, and perhaps, help both their worlds.

"Step back with me, *Ya'lenali*, step back into your memory, watch your past become unveiled. Watch with me as all is revealed. See all that moved, hear all that was spoken, scent each aroma, and taste even the air." As Asler spoke the ritual, he slid Susan back into deep *m'ittar*, past the point they had so far experienced and into a place where he could change the form of her memory. Slowly he pulled her psyche from the memories, changing her perception of the past as though she merely watched, rather than experienced, each moment of her time on the terrorist ship.

"Everything is black," Susan whispered.

"Step forward with me, and see, Susan Branscombe." Asler spoke into her mind.

Together they moved forward into the memory. The darkness took on a dim light, and the air grew rancid. In the shadows they could see a body collapsed flat on the floor.

Susan let go of his hand and stepped closer.

"That's me." Her mental voice shook slightly, but the *m'ittar* contact held.

Asler released the breath he had been holding as he realized he had still maintained an unconscious fear that she would reject the process and use her untrained power to throw them both from the memory before anything at all could be revealed. They would have tried again, but each unsuccessful try would mean less possibility of success.

"It is you, as you were when you were first captured. What do you see?" Asler prompted. Much of what could be gleaned from these memories would have to come from her as she understood more of the context. The terrorists were human, and she was human. Their ship would be more familiar, their languages and their technology. Asler would watch for anything he recognized. Anything that registered with him as familiar would be significant, as it would prove an alien influence.

Together they would find something.

"I see some blood, a minor head wound. It's too dark, I can't see any evidence of being drugged." She stepped closer, stared down at herself.

"What about the room?" He distracted her, not expecting anything from the redirection. Asler knew from experience that she should not look too closely at her own injuries.

She peered into the shadows. *"No, there's nothing..."* Her voice faded away as the sound of footsteps approached. She jumped back to grab at him as the door slammed open. The body on the ground groaned and shuddered slightly as two large men entered the cell.

"She's coming around." The harsh voice spoke in standard English, but Asler noted something different about its accent. The man didn't sound like any of the humans he had been exposed to thus far.

"Good enough. Let's take her down to Gerish. The sooner he finds out the location, the sooner we'll end this thing. There's no way we're gonna let some creepy-crawly alien bastard take over our planet. We've got to stop 'em now." He reached down to haul the semi-conscious Susan from the floor. She struggled in his arms, managing to elbow him solidly in the solar-plexus. In return he backhanded her in the face.

In the shadows, the psychic form of Susan touched her face where her body had been struck.

"Why do they sound different?" Asler caught her hand and held it. They watched the two men drag Susan's body out into the hall, eventually following them into the ships corridors. Asler scanned the walls closely, but found no markings of any kind.

"They're from the Soviets, I think. You hear an accent, a tinge of their local dialect." Distracted, Susan said, *"They sound guttural because of it. Look at that."* She pointed to the doorway the men had just entered. Writing painted on the grey walls in red indicated dangerous materials inside, but the warning had been marked over with an X. *"That's Starforce standard code."* Susan scanned the walls more closely. *"Some of this ship has been salvaged from Starforce."* Thoughtfully, she pursed her lips. *"I don't think this ship was engineered for a particular group. I think it's a junker—a ship forged from scavenged materials by those who can't afford to build new."*

They stepped into the room, observing Susan's body being unceremoniously dumped in a chair. Then the two captors stood aside, waiting for a new man to enter. Tall and whipcord thin, the new man stalked to Susan and grabbed her chin.

"She is not fully conscious." He let her head drop. "I need her to be awake to answer questions, idiots." He drew back a hand and brought it down hard against Susan's face in a stinging slap.

Her moan of anguish was duplicated as her psyche, watching from the doorway, moaned as well.

"That's enough." Asler said. *"Step back into the present, Susan. That's enough."*

He held her as they returned to his room, held her as she sobbed in his arms. "That's the man. That's the man who tortured me."

"I know. But we did it, *Ya'lenali*. We watched a memory and learned something." He waited until the sobs slowly subsided.

"Yes…"

She fell silent.

Asler tipped her head up gently to look at her, and it was only then that he realized that she had succumbed to exhaustion.

SUE OPENED HER EYES. The room was bathed in a deep red glow. As she slowly became more awake, she realized she lay in Asler's bed. Curiously, the lightweight coverlet seemed to be exuding the light, along with mild warmth. Far more interestingly, the naked skin of the man beside her radiated a deep heat that begged for touch. She stared openly at him, the man who had taken over most of her life. He dominated her every waking moment, had taken over her past and, she suspected, would play a key role in her future.

She had never met anyone quite like him. He was determined to find the truth, insistent in his duty, but still remained kind—even mentally giving her clothing when she felt her most insecure at facing the memories of her torture. He was highly sensual, yet his physique and his bearing hinted at being familiar with hard work.

Sue lifted her fingers to touch his long dark hair. The

reddish hue of his *L'inar* markings as they wound along his neck and shoulders reminded her of old photos she'd seen of tribal tattoos. As she watched they rippled, rising slightly then lowering flat against his skin once again. No, he certainly was not like anyone she had ever met in her life. He wasn't human.

And, she realized, she didn't care. She had already come to care for the man. In only a matter of days she had gone from caring more about her career than her life to caring more about a man than her career.

Hell. I will do my duty, I will find out the truth and protect the Treaty. But when that is over…

She watched his *L'inar* lines ripple again.

When that is over I will learn everything about m'ittar. Earth won't want me, not if I can't prove without a doubt that I am innocent, and even then my career will likely be over. But maybe I can still help. Maybe I can be an Examiner or an ambassador. Maybe I can work with Asler, stay with him.

She shivered as the ideas and feelings flowed though her—amazement, excitement, yearning, desire.

Asler slept on, his heavy chest rising and falling beside her. She nudged him slightly. Nothing, no response came from his muscular frame, even as she poked him a little harder. *A sound sleeper.*

Taking advantage of the moment, Sue pulled back the light coverlet. Leaning up on her elbows she stared at Asler's strong body. His *L'inar* stirred, the ridges undulating slightly. Without volition her fingers rose to trace them lightly. The crests lifted, firming slightly to her touch, although not rising to their full height. She couldn't help it, couldn't resist lowering her lips to kiss the line covering his hip with a sinuous curve.

Would a kiss be enough to tell an inarrii she wanted him? Was there such a thing as bunkmates, or was it an all-or-nothing marriage deal? She licked her lips, glancing up at his face. *Still asleep.* Delicately she ran her tongue over the curving line of skin.

Licking the *L'inar*, she delighted in the way it reacted and rose.

She kissed the ridge again. After only a few inches it broke into several lines, some stretching across the lowest part of his abdomen, some curving back toward his back and buttocks. Some of the lines beckoned as they traced a dancing path toward his most private areas.

I can't do this. To him, this could be like a marriage proposal, and I don't even know how he feels.

Sue groaned and rolled onto her back.

"Don't stop, Ya'lenali."

Sue glanced over to meet Asler's bright green eyes. "What do you keep calling me?" Her voice sounded low and husky to her ears.

He rolled onto his side and reached for her, stroked lazy fingers down her arm. "What does your heart tell you it means?"

"Something...something special."

"Yes," he breathed. He touched her jaw line, cradled her face in one large hand. His mouth opened and Sue knew, absolutely knew with a pulse of excitement that raced the length of her spine and zeroed in on her heart, that whatever he was about to say would change her life forever.

A low chime invaded the moment. Neither of them moved, but she saw his eyes flicker.

"What is it?" Sue turned from him and mentally shook herself. Thank God for the interruption. What had she been thinking? What had she done? She hoped like hell he had been too asleep to sense completely how she had tasted his *L'inar.* Hoped too that she had not gone far enough to make any promises. Her future was too cloudy to know what she could offer.

Asler looked troubled, his brows drawing together. "There is someone who wishes to see us."

Sue drew up the coverlet. She still wore the *pettan* and *pet-horin* top, but felt exposed. *Pull it together, Branscombe.*

You've been in the forces long enough not to freak over a run in with some Brass. A part of her began to sweat. For the first time she thought of how things would look to a Starforce observer. She was fraternizing with the very person meant to evaluate her innocence. How would that look to anyone? *Whoever is here to see Asler will know I've been in his bed. Hell, his commander already knew. What would my base commander think if he saw us like this?*

She flipped off the cover and bounced out of the bed, moving to the bedroom wall. "Are they in the office?" She flushed as she realized her voice had squeaked as she spoke.

"No, they are in the hall…"

Sue didn't wait for Asler to finish the sentence, let alone rise from the bed. She was out the bedroom door and across the office to the lavatory before the chime sounded again. She waved her hand across the wall after she shut herself into the room. As Asler had shown her, the wall's surface morphed to show her a visual of herself. *Damn, I look like I went a round with a boxer and then slept with him.* An unnoticed bruise had formed on her cheek, likely resulting from some action she'd performed while fighting the fire in the dining room. Her tousled hair seemed to scream out the fact that she'd been flat on her back in Asler's bed. Her cheeks were flushed.

Quickly she pawed through the storage shelves looking for a brush. Nothing. *How the hell does he comb that long hair of his? What the hell is all this stuff?* Nothing seemed familiar. In frustration she jammed her fingers through her short blonde locks.

Sue listened hard, but she couldn't hear anything happening in the office. She bit her lip. *Might as well face whoever it is out there.*

She palmed the door open and peeked out into the office.

Oh shit.

. . .

ASLER SHRUGGED into the heavy *chammiss* robes under the affronted glare of the human Base Commander John Davies. Obviously a *pettan* was not enough for the man, and Asler mentally congratulated the anthropological findings of the first team to observe the humans. They'd been right about the clothing.

"Stay calm, Kiis." Asler's Commander Jannii Finar gently reminded him. *"Commander Davies is very worried about Captain Branscombe."* Jannii stood to one side, his calm appearance in direct contrast to Davies's outraged one.

"Just what is going on here? Where is my Captain?"

Asler spied the lavatory door crack open. When Susan didn't immediately step out, he realized she might be dreading any confrontation with a man she equalized to a father. "Captain Branscombe is, as I believe you put it, indisposed. I am certain she will be back in a moment."

"She'd better be. I knew I was right to insist Admiral Jeffers get me in here." Davies crossed his arms in front of his chest. His steel grey eyes bore into Asler's and seemed to imply that Asler could not take care of the girl.

"Commander Davies, we have codes, just as you do, about the treatment of anyone in our care," Asler explained to the distraught man. "Captain Branscombe has not been harmed. She has been completely healed from the harm inflicted upon her by the terrorists. She has cooperated with us fully. We have already begun to learn some things about her captors."

"Hrumph. I'll reserve my opinions on all that until I see her."

A movement at the edge of Asler's vision caught his attention. Susan had stepped out of the lavatory. She met his eyes and hesitated before joining the conversation.

"Commander Davies." She approached the group, her spine stiffly erect as she stopped and gave a quick salute.

"Captain Branscombe. Where is your uniform?" The commander's voice sounded clipped to Asler's ears, and a flush stained Susan's cheeks into high spots of red.

It's a good thing I had the pet-horin for her to wear and that she had them on for this little visit.

"Indeed it is." The Inarrii commander interjected into his mind. Asler immediately clamped down on his mental control, shocked that he had leaked so much of his private thoughts for anyone to hear.

He looked at Jannii and caught the ghost of a wry smile on the corner of his mouth.

"I'm sorry sir…"

"None were available immediately upon her healing, Commander," Asler interjected, bringing the human's attention back to him. "She has only been out of the MedTech care for the last thirty six of your hours. There has been little time to request one."

"That will be immediately rectified, Examiner," the base commander told him coldly. He looked back at Susan, his gaze raking her from head to toe.

"I thought you said she had been healed completely? Why does she have a bruise on her face? And her knuckles are scraped."

Susan glanced down at her hands and then looked at Asler. *"Should I tell him about the attack?"*

Asler's heart thudded hard. She'd actively sent him a thought. He glanced at Jannii and saw the shock in his face. He'd caught the message as well. Susan had nearly no shielding yet, something Asler would have to correct soon.

"Well?" Commander Davies was clearly unimpressed by the silence, his concern and suspicion evident as he glared at each of them in turn.

"Commander Davies," Jannii took the lead, "I must ask that what you hear now is held in the strictest of confidence. Very few of your people are aware that we have been attacked since the initial strike by the terrorist group Terran Purity. We have kept it quiet for several security reasons. Captain Branscombe was onboard and involved in the latest attack, risking herself to aid us in the case of a shipboard fire."

"What the hell? Who attacked you? The Terrorists again?" Davies put his hands on his hips, his fists clenched tight. He looked ready for a fight, and Asler was struck again by the assertive nature of the man. *This is what Susan respects in him.*

"That is one of the largest security concerns. We are attempting to discern the identity of the attackers, but it does appear as though someone of nonhuman origin may be involved. Captain Branscombe's memories will hopefully be able to give us some evidence in that matter."

Asler took Susan's hand in his, examining the scrapes on her knuckles. He hadn't noticed them, or the bruise on her cheek, in the soft red light of his private chambers. For that alone he was sorry. "We will have this fixed immediately."

She pulled away from him, her cheeks flaming. "It's nothing." She looked at her Base commander. "I'm fine. I was close to the damaged area when the attack hit. It was a serious assault. People were badly injured."

"What progress have you made in recovering any information from your memories?" Davies's voice, while demanding, contained a hint of the emotion Asler could sense surging inside him. Concern and pride for his officer leaked out to reach Asler's mind. He warmed to the older man, recognizing the emotions as those of a father.

Susan, still somewhat stiff in her bearing, replied, "Examiner Kiis and I have managed what they call *m'ittar,* a kind of mind contact. We are reviewing my…time in captivity." She paused, grimaced. "The terrorists had accents, tones of the Soviets. The ship was a junker, which I am sure you already know if you have been looking at what is left of it. There were even bits salvaged from old Starforce ships. You might be able to track part of that—I saw a door plate with markings from the SS Alure. The leader, or at least the chief torturer, went by the name Gerish. That's all I have for now."

Commander Davies nodded. "That's more than I

expected. We'll get started with that from our end." He turned to Asler. "Has enough been discovered to clear her?"

"Captain Branscombe cannot be released until the investigation is complete and a report is made to the Confederacy board for judgment," the Inarrii commander interjected.

"Very well. I would like a few minutes with my officer alone."

"We cannot leave her with you, but we can offer you some privacy." Asler gestured to the side of the office, where the wall curved over the low couch. He and Jannii stepped aside to the desk, leaving as much space between them and the humans as possible without leaving the room.

He watched as the humans sat close together on the couch. Davies leaned in to Susan, whispered something in her ear. Susan nodded, whispered back, and then shook her head vehemently at something the commander whispered to her. Davies stood, clasped her on the shoulder, and made a final hushed comment. Susan's lips pressed together tightly, but she nodded.

"I will return now to make my report to Admiral Jeffers. I am sure you will understand, but I must report everything I heard here, although I will explain the need for discretion." Davies addressed both of the Inarrii, but his eyes were focused on Asler. "I will expect a further report soon, both on any information retrieved, and on Captain Branscombe's condition."

"Thank you, Base Commander Davies," Asler replied smoothly. "I would ask that in return that you forward any information you discover on the junker ship's manufacture. Susan herself will vidcon a report to you after our next session." The suspicion had returned to Davies's eyes, and he wished he could reduce the man's tension. If nothing else, the tension had passed to Susan, and between the two humans, Asler was getting a headache.

. . .

SUE REMAINED SEATED as she watched her commander exit the office. He hadn't looked back at her. The meeting had left her shaken, and tiny tremors ran down her back.

She looked at Asler, still staring at the doorway. She expected he was still in mind contact with his own commander. She made a mild effort to listen for their conversation but quickly gave it up as useless. She shook her head at the ridiculousness of the situation. Asler might believe she had powers, but in the light of day she had a hard time imagining that was true. She rolled her shoulders, trying to reduce the tension in her body.

Davies's whispered words still rang in her ears. *"Are you really okay? I've heard things…Has anyone tried to…do anything?"* She'd seen the implication in his eyes. Dear God, how could he know that she'd slept with an alien? The naughty side of her interjected, *Could he possibly have imagined how very much you liked it or wanted it to continue?*

Sue looked up to find Asler's eyes on her. No wonder her commander had speculated about their involvement. Alser had left his hair hanging loose in a dark cascade down his back. Although he had hastily donned his official robes, they were poorly tied, and she caught a glimpse of his bronzed skin just below the neckline. She smoldered just looking at him, her skin heating as she imagined what lay beneath his robes. How could anyone miss her reaction to him?

Her commander's parting words hissed though her memory. *"Get through this. Find out what you can, and then we'll get you back where you belong, with Starforce."*

But she'd hesitated before agreeing with him, her body rebelling before it finally nodded acceptance. With shock she realized that a part of her did not want to go back.

Asler approached her, reached out a hand to touch her hair, but she shied away.

"We need to get through those memories." She told him, quietly. "No more delays."

He didn't say anything for a moment, just looked at her with those startling green eyes. Then he held out his hand to her. "Don't pull away, Susan. It will make our *m'ittar* more difficult. And...I would miss you."

She took his hand, let her pull him up against him. *Why fight it?* Her inner self whispered. *You have so little time left with him. Enjoy it.* She gave in, leaned against him and pressed her lips to the patch of skin she'd glimpsed earlier.

He held her. Since she had woken from the nightmare of torture and found herself healed, this had been what he offered her. Safety, trust, caring. She'd felt secure in the Starforce after her parents died, respected and liked. But never like this. It was no wonder she couldn't resist when he kissed her. That she gave in to her desire. What Davies had implied—improper conduct, at the least—wasn't important. *Was it?*

"You have to relax." Asler's deep voice rumbled in her ears. "I can sense conflict in you." He lowered her back to the couch and pulled the *pet-horin* from her shoulders and over her head. "Lie down."

"We don't have time, really," she murmured. But she lay down on the padded couch, enjoying the heat that immediately rose from its cushions to cradle her back.

"Just relax. And roll over." He smiled at her, laughter smothered by the deep tone of his rich voice.

She rolled to her stomach. He swept aside her hair and began to rub her back in circular motions, the warmth of his hands easily outdoing that of the cushions beneath her. She moaned as he worked the stress from her muscles. "My god, that feels good."

"Someday we will have to talk about your god." Asler commented. "But now it is time to step back into your memories." *"Relax and step back. Do not be afraid, I am here with you. We are together seeing what happened, not what is happening.*

This is the past. See it, hear it, smell it, taste it, we are together in what has already happened."

The tension eased from her. When Asler's mind reached for hers it was akin to clasping hands. She felt the contact, the joining.

And then they were back. Sue looked at her body as it had been, her face reddened and bruised from Gerish's slap.

"You're awake. Listen carefully. You will tell me the answer to anything I ask. If you do not answer truthfully and immediately, I will hurt you. Do you understand?"

Sue stared at the terrorist, her eyes wide as she took in where she was and what was being said. When she didn't answer immediately, Gerish casually picked up her left hand and snapped the bone in her smallest finger. She cried out.

"Don't forget, Susan, that this is the past."

Sue flinched as Asler reminded her. She looked away from the pain in her own eyes.

"Look around, do you see anything more here that can tell us anything?"

"No. Wait. I hear something. I hear...a voice in the corridor."

She stepped toward the door, and Asler moved with her. *"I can't see—the door is half shut and it is dark out there."*

"Someone was watching you."

"Yes. Gerish is not the one in charge, although he might think he is."

A scream cut the air. They turned back to see Susan's index finger snap in Gerish's cruel grasp. "Take her back to the cell." He told the watching guards. "Give her a reminder about why she had best answer my questions soon. I want the location of those alien pigs."

Susan was picked up roughly and thrown over the shoulder of the larger of the two men. They stomped through the door and into the corridor with Susan and Asler's astral beings close on their heels.

"Damn, I couldn't see who was here. But they were really tall. Taller than you." Sue directed her thoughts at Asler.

"Not many humans are this size, are they?"

Sue didn't bother to answer. They couldn't see things when her body hadn't been there to experience it in some minor way, so they followed the guards to the holding cell. Quietly they watched Sue sob as she took repeated blows to her ribs and legs from the guard's crushing boots.

"Look away," Asler pleaded with her.

"No. This is what happened to me. I remember it all. Those bastards loved to kick."

The memory faded to black. Before Sue could comment, the light returned, and she found herself again watching Gerish as her body sat helplessly before him, force bindings holding her to the same rough metal chair.

Chapter 9

"There is no way to know how many memories you have like this, Susan. We may learn nothing at all other than the extent of their brutality. I am sorry." Asler's heart ached as he watched Susan clench her jaw. Her determination to watch events unfold with him illuminated her strength but also her pride. How much could she take in one session?

"Today, you little bitch, you will tell us everything you know. We will attack those filthy alien Inarrii and wipe out this sacrilegious agreement before it ever comes to pass. We will attack their ships, Starforce whore, or we will attack the Starforce training camp. We will prevent Earths' children from ever coming into contact with those foul creatures." Gerish raved fanatically at his prisoner, constantly pacing in front of Susan and frantically scratching the back of his neck as he did so.

"There. Look at my face, now, while no one else can see. This is the moment I decided to tell them." Susan's face mirrored the anguish on the face of her memory.

"You told them our location."

"I had to, or they would have attached the Starforce schools. There were children there. He meant it, Asler." Susan faced him, her mouth grim. "See the way he keeps scratching? He's using a drug called Slam. It increases strength, stamina, even the speed of *thought, but it has some pretty bad side effects. It'll make him itch 'til he scratches his skin off in places. It also ensures that you say every-thing that you mean. He would kill anyone to make his point."*

Gerish pulled a laser torch from his greasy shipsuit pant pocket. He smiled as he fired it up, waving the microbeam dangerously close to Susan's face. "Tell me! Where is the ship? Where are they meeting?"

Susan's screams tore through the air as Gerish pointed the beam against the fabric of the dirty uniform stretching across her leg. Burning flesh produced an odor Asler had hoped to never smell again.

"Stop! Stop! I'll tell you, please, please stop!" The figure of Susan's memory begged.

"This is it. This is where I turned a traitor."

"No. Look at your eye, remember your face earlier. You had to wait to tell them, until it became so unbelievably painful that they would have to believe. You waited on purpose. Why?"

Asler pulled Susan close and looked into her eyes. He already believed her innocence; now she needed to believe in herself.

"I...I waited so they would believe and go for it—attack the meeting. I knew there would be at least three of our ships there, as well as yours. I couldn't believe men like these could have enough resources to succeed in doing much damage to that kind of a meeting. But if they attacked the Starforce school...there are children there, and not much in the way of defense. I grew up there."

Asler saw the acceptance in her eyes. *"You did what you had to, to save as many as you could."*

"Yes."

Susan turned back to watch herself sobbing the coordi-nates of the meeting out to her torturer. Smoke curled up from the wound on her thigh. The injured woman barely looked up as another presence entered the room, but Asler caught Susan stiffen beside him, heard her soft gasp of surprise.

A tall, lanky man, the newcomer wasn't someone that Asler recognized, but what he saw around his neck was as clear as crystal. If he could have ripped it from the grinning man's neck he would have in a heartbeat.

"Flight Lieutenant Cohen! I can't believe he's a part of this!"

"I don't believe he is, Susan. Take this moment, this memory, and with me, stop it. Hold it still, Susan." Movement ceased around them, the image of the memory warping for a moment as Susan struggled to work with Asler's mental commands.

Asler walked closer to the newcomer terrorist. A glowing band of metal circled tight to his throat. He pointed it out to Susan. *"This is a Gathan invention, a kind of portable disguise. It projects an image tightly to the body of the wearer, nearly undetectable except for the unit itself."*

"You mean that's not Cohen?"

"I'd have to say no. Considering the height, I'd say that probably isn't even a human. Likely a Gathan—a blue skinned race that the Confederacy rejected not long ago. They don't share their technology easily. The terrorists probably didn't even know it, but they have been working with the Ravagers. And now we have proof."

The memory began to flow around them again, and together they watched as Susan was forced to repeat her information again and again. The Gathan watched everything carefully but never said a word. Finally Susan was dragged back to her cell. This time there was no beating, just a sharp push into a wall, and then she was left to collapse onto the floor and sob her grief out.

"Susan, the door isn't quite shut," Asler pointed it out to her, but he could feel her flow of emotion. She had known it was open, even when she had been held captive.

"I know. I saw it then. I might have escaped. But…"

"Yes? What stopped you? Why didn't you run?"

"Does it really matter?"

"You know it does." He reached out to clasp her hand with his.

"I thought that if I were here, I might be able to stop them, to do something from inside." Susan paced inside the cell, so near the image of her memory self.

"There is more." Asler led her as his training dictated—to the truth.

"No, I'd told them the truth and they would die from it, attacking a target they couldn't hope to win against. I would sabotage them."

"More," Asler insisted.

"I was hurt…and I knew if I were caught they would hurt me more. I was…afraid."

"You couldn't move for the fear, could you?"

"No," she choked out. *"It was everywhere, and I was drowning in it."* Her thoughts were raged, the sensation of them raw to Asler's senses. He opened himself to her, wrapped her trembling psyche into his arms. Facing the truth about herself, this was the ultimate form of bravery. In that moment he held her, he faced his own truth. The emotion he had been avoiding in himself radiated over them both.

He loved her.

SUE OPENED her eyes to the bland color and curving shape of Asler's office ceiling. She glanced around, but the room stood empty, save her and the simple low couches. Even his desk had disappeared into the wall. Asler's discarded robe covered her, its gentle warmth scented with Asler's unique aroma. She pressed her face to it, reveled in the moment. They had found what they needed to prove the Ravager involvement in the terrorist attacks. Success gave her back some of the pride she'd lost, and the truth freed her, at least from her personal guilt over not trying to escape.

Sue sat up, shivering slightly as she left the warmth of the heated couch. The unpleasant sensation travelled to her stomach. They had proved the outside involvement, but had they proved her innocence?

She stood and walked to the lavatory. It too stood empty. The lack of noise, something she hadn't noticed before, seemed to reverberate in her ears. She opened the cupboard that had housed the clothing she had borrowed earlier, but could only find more *pettan* coverings. She pulled on a fresh set and, uncertain what to do with her old one, left it on the floor near the ultrasonic cleanser.

She walked back through the office and to the bedroom, hesitating at the doorway. A tingle of desire swept through her, and her lips curved as thoughts of the satisfaction she had achieved here slipped through her mind. Her smile faded. She'd almost gone too far here as well. Almost.

She wandered back to the office and nearly sat down on the coach again, then stood uncertainly. Her stomach growled. At least that was something she could do. Years onboard ships had taught her to remember each step, and she was fairly certain she could find the dining room again. She'd almost reached the door when she hesitated again. *Do I really want to go back there alone?* She could feel the heat rising in her face. *Do single people even go there?*

She pressed her lips together. This wasn't like her. She was hungry, she would go and get something to eat. God knew she had no idea how to work Asler's desk, and that was where he had ordered food in the room.

She stepped up to the door and waited for the scanner to recognize her as it had when she had gone out with Asler. When nothing happened, she waved her hand in front of the scanner. The equipment stayed silent.

Sue's throat constricted. She was still considered a prisoner. With a sigh, she retuned to the couch and wrapped herself again in Asler's discarded robe, cuddling into it like a blanket for its warmth, and she admitted to herself for the comfort his scent offered to her.

"Asler," she called out to him with her mind. She waited but there was no answer, not even the warm presence of his mind.

She shook her head. Who was she kidding? The only contact she'd achieved with him was when she was right there in his gentle arms.

Sue slumped down on the couch, held her head in her

hands. She didn't move when the door slid open, didn't even look up until she heard the crack of her commander's voice.

"Captain Branscombe! Attention, officer on deck."

Sue leapt to attention, her head snapping forward as she peripherally took in the appearance of Base Commander Davies, Asler and his Commander Jannii Finar at the door. Her heart beat a rapid tattoo as she realized belatedly that she had dropped the robe and now stood in only her *pettan*.

Immediately she flushed from the roots of her hair to the tips of her breasts.

"This! This is exactly what I was afraid of." Her commander growled as he paced forward and picked up the robe to cover her exposed body.

"Captain Branscombe has not been mistreated in any way." Finar stated calmly.

"Perhaps not in your understanding, but going around half dressed in public goes against our moral codes," Davies ranted. "Besides, you can't tell me that there is nothing going on between Captain Branscombe and Kiis. It's written all over them. That is not allowed in the Starforce Marines. Branscombe has been trained to obey all commands by her superiors—it's the chain of command. If she's been coerced by your Examiner acting as her superior, Starforce considers that a form of rape."

"Susan has not been coerced!" Asler crowded the Base Commander, the two men facing off in the confines of the office and nearly knocking Sue over. "She has been physically healed, and we have been investigating her memories for the truth, as well as healing the damage done to her psyche."

"I think she's had quite enough of your kind of healing." Davies leaned in toward the enraged Inarrii, his fisted hands like loaded weapons ready at his sides.

Sue's stomach dropped. Nausea washed over her. The most important men in her life were going to kill each other, right in front of her. Not only would the Treaty come to a screeching halt, Sue thought her heart would as well.

"Sir," she began, her voice shaky.

"Not a word, Branscombe, until we get you to our own people. This interrogation is over." Davies grabbed her arm, nearly dragging her from the room.

Commander Finar stood aside and let them leave, staring pointedly at Asler's fuming face. Sue hoped he was mentally commanding the man to stand down before things went too far.

"It will be okay," she sent to Asler as she stepped into the corridor.

"WHAT JUST HAPPENED?" Asler demanded. "Why are we letting him take her? After all I just told you?" He paced the office, wishing for once that it were bigger. His briefing with Finar had been interrupted by the arrival of the suspicious human base commander, but there had been enough time to describe the involvement of the Gathan and the likely involvement of the Ravagers in the recent terrorist attacks. "I thought the Confederacy was in complete control of the investigation."

Finar watched him pace, his features calm. *"We have what we need in regard to the Ravager involvement. And I believe you have enough memories to present Captain Branscombe's state of mind during her captivity and the reasoning behind her disclosure of information."*

"She barely had time to admit her own fear. There is no way for her to heal like this. We must get her back."

"You care for her. I am sorry, but the negotiations are at a very delicate stage, really just the beginning of the most important agreements. We must let her return to her Starforce."

"They won't understand."

Finar laid a hand on his shoulder. *"A formal trial will be held later this week, and your findings will be presented in written format. We will be able to observe. Her people will surely take care of her, Asler."*

Finar left the office. Asler resisted an uncharacteristic urge to rip the place apart as he continued to pace. Susan might be physically safe with her people, but she would not heal. She'd barely admitted her fear, and she had yet to truly deal with the torture she'd experienced. Now she faced the human's questions and would no longer have a complete set of memories – those that they had observed would no longer be the same. How would she explain that? How could she answer without him beside her?

A soft chime rang at the office door. Asler ignored it. The only person he longed to see would already be on her way to the Starforce Base on Earth.

The chime rang again.

With a snarl, Asler opened the door, only to face a concerned friend, Co-Examiner Salis. Asler turned his back on the concert, marching once again the length of his office.

"You must calm down, Asler. We can hear you all over the ship." Salis stepped inside the room and shut the door.

Asler stopped mid-step. He looked over his shoulder at Salis. *He is telling the truth. I must stop.* He sat slowly on the low couch and took a deep breath. "This is intolerable. They have taken Susan back to Earth to answer questions about memories she may no longer even have."

"You initiated *m'ittar densah*?" Salis sat as well, facing him from the second couch. "Was it truly necessary?"

"Her pain was too great, and we needed to see clearly any clue that the Ravagers might be involved in the attacks."

"I'm sorry I haven't been here for you. I have been attending the Treaty talks."

Asler grimaced. "Better you than me."

"All this vocality is tiring. Has your human charge convinced you to live so orally? Or is that just a benefit of such a beautiful woman?"

Salis leered at him, clearly trying to lighten Asler's spirits with his version of humor.

Asler sighed. It all came back to Susan. He couldn't release the tension from his body. Broad bands of it held him tightly even in the company of an old friend. *"You've been talking to Commander Finar."*

Salis leaned forward, the smile disappearing from his face. *"Yes, I have. You've become attached to this woman."*

"She is incredible. Brave, beyond what I had expected, intelligent, loyal, and highly sensual. She has talents in m'ittar that are completely unpredicted in humans."

"That is a concern, Asler. Both that you have become so attached and that she has wild m'ittar. Are you completely certain of her innocence?"

Asler's lips pressed tightly together as anger pulsed through his *l'inar*. "She is *Ya'lenali.*"

Salis leaned back, his features once again relaxing. "So you have made your choice. I wish you well. If she is your intended, well, we'll get her back. Have you performed *M'itta lensahn?*"

Asler's shoulders relaxed as his friend spoke about the ritual mating without any sense of judgment. Salis's easy acceptance of his choice and his offer to help meant many things, not the least of which was likely acceptance of a human as mate by most of the Inarrii.

"Not yet. It was amazing though. She doesn't really understand, but she actually initiated the beginning herself. I had told her some of the meaning of the *l'inar*, and she understood what she was offering, at least on some level." He ran a hand across his jaw. The *l'inar* along the sides of his face had risen slightly at the thought of Susan's actions in bed, when she had thought he was asleep.

Salis laughed. "You are looking a little heated, my friend."

"Someday, when you have made your choice, I will be there for you, my *friend*. I need her. And I am afraid. She has no one to protect her."

Chapter 10

S ue shivered as a chill passed through her. Despite the fact that she was now fully clothed in her uniform, she felt exposed and cold under the watchful eyes of the Starforce Inquiries Board and the guards they seemed to feel were necessary. Her chill matched the uneasy sensation of frustration that was quickly building inside her as they asked the same questions again and again

"Who is the leader of the terrorist group Terran Purity? Who held you captive?" The questions came again. They seemed to be getting as frustrated as she was. "What is your involvement with the group?"

"I am not involved with any terrorist group. I am a loyal member of Starforce. I was held against my will and tortured."

"Describe the terrorist leader." This was where the trouble began again. Asler had been right, some of the memories were damaged, some scrambled.

"I'm not sure. He hurt me..."

"We are aware of the extent of your injuries, Captain Branscombe. The question is when did you receive them, before or after your told them the location of the first Treaty talks?" demanded a young lawyer. He banged his fist against the table as he spoke, his impatience growing with the volume of his voice.

She missed the quiet of the alien ship, the peace in Asler's arms.

"Your attention, Captain Branscombe! Describe again what it is that you *can* remember, please."

"I'm sorry. As I mentioned, when As...Examiner Kiis and I reviewed the memories using his process of *m'ittar*, it changed some, and even removed some. I *can't* describe those things."

She tried to remain calm as she spoke. This was the third day of questioning, and everyone, herself included, were growing tired of the same responses. She couldn't give them answers – those had been left behind with Asler.

If I could just go back...

"Let's go back to your time with the Inarrii," a newcomer commented.

Sue looked up at his tone. Something was off with the way he twisted his lips. She had seen him attending yesterday, but this was the first time he'd spoken. She didn't recognize the insignia he wore.

"I've had some recent information about this *m'ittar*." Sue stiffened at the tone of his voice as he continued. "I've had detailed reports on the mind contact and how the Inarrii use physical contact to smooth the way, so to speak."

"I don't know what you mean," she said, her voice as cold as the chill racing again down her back.

"I understand you were practically nude when we collected you from the Inarrii ship Horneu. That you were confined to quarters with Kiis the entire time you were onboard."

Rage chased away the chill Sue had been feeling. Only the base commander had known that. How could he have exposed her this way? Davies hadn't attended any of the hearing so far. Perhaps this was why.

Her heart pounded. "Aside from the two days I spent in the medical lab healing from *torture*, that is correct."

Murmurs raced through the board. They were frustrated at the lack of progress in this investigation; would they now take this out on her in a different way? For the first time, Sue felt frightened. The Inarrii and their understanding of sex was different than that of the general populace of Earth. It seemed that no matter how far Earth advanced, the differences in the sexes and the importance of the male/female relationship were points of contention.

The annoying man stood. "So, you were alone with an Inarrii male, attempting mind contact to review the very memories you claim to no longer be able to access. He claims you are innocent of any involvement with the terrorists, and has made a report to this council to that effect." He paced closer to where Sue sat facing the Board. "Tell me, Captain, you were pretty good at giving the terrorists information, and evidently Kiis was…satisfied by you. What have you got for us? Nothing but claims of broken memories."

Sue bounced to her feet. "How dare you. I have done nothing wrong! I told the terrorists where the sips were meeting, but only because I felt certain that we could defeat them. And because if they didn't know, they would have chosen some other target, one less able to defend itself!"

"What target?" He stood face to face with her.

"I don't know! I can't remember," she cried out, tears of anger and frustration threatening to spill from her eyes.

"Did you have sex with them?" he yelled. "Did you fuck the terrorists and then the Inarrii to gain favors? I hope it was good, Captain, because it's over now."

She lunged at him, her nerves broken. Anger had pushed here where fear and frustration couldn't. She grabbed the man but before she could strike him, the guards were on her.

"Take her away," he said, his face calm. "In our next

round of questioning, we won't be as patient as we have been." He turned away from her and looked at the Starforce officers attending the inquiry. "We need answers, gentlemen," he addressed the Board, some of whom were now on their feet in alarm. "The Earth Council has given me the authority to disband the Board here and take control of this investigation. We need answers faster than you are going to get them, if you ever do. I will now be using a different method. You will be allowed to attend, if you feel the need, but I have every power to conduct an inquiry in any method deemed necessary. Are we clear?"

Sue struggled as the guard applied force bindings. Her mind rebelled. *Not again!* She couldn't stand it again—not this, not torture. Some of her memories were gone, scrambled past repair, but she clearly remembered the pain, the desperation to make it stop.

She collapsed as the guards began to drag her. *"Asler!"* Her mind called for the only man she felt safe with.

ASLER SLAMMED his hand against the force barrier separating him from the inquiry. "How can they allow this?" he demanded to Salis. His Co-Examiner stood beside him, along with Commander Finar and the human emissary, Starforce Major David Brown. "Look at her, she's terrified." He couldn't drag his eyes from Susan as she was brutally taken into custody.

"They must have answers, Examiner Kiis. The presence of an agent of the Starforce Intelligence Department is very serious."

"We have to stop this. I can hear her fear. She is calling out for me and is terrified they will harm her. I don't think she can stand to go through this again, Major Brown. Her mind is very raw at this point. Despite her bravery, we'd only begun to heal her." Asler's voice broke on the words. He shook his head at the grave expression on the human officer's face.

"There is nothing we can do. It is only because of the Treaty that you can be here to observe at all. Diplomatic immunity is all that keeps you from being questioned as well, Examiner Kiis. Your position is tenuous at best."

"Commander Finar," Asler address his friend and commander, *"We must do something. It was because of my choice of method that Susan cannot retrieve the memories that would now clear her name. She cannot answer their questions. Please, I will do anything. I will undergo questioning myself as to what was observed. You know very well that my word should be all that is needed to find her innocent."*

Susan was being dragged away, collapsing against the guard's grasp, her arms in force-bindings. Her mind reached out and called out his name.

Asler slammed his hand again on the force barrier. He caught Finar's quick gasp. "You heard her, didn't you? She has *m'ittar*, strong enough to call out to everyone in the city, I'd bet. Her mind will be broken, that resource lost. We must save her."

Finar broke the silence he'd maintained throughout the inquiry and Asler's rant. "Yes, we must." He stared at Asler. "Are you truly ready for the ramifications of being questioned on this matter? If your own memories are exposed, you may be forced to abandon your entire career before this is over."

"I'm ready."

"I hope so. What we do now may change everything." Finar turned to the human emissary. "Major Brown, I hope you will accompany us. We must return to the ship and speak with our own council before we interrupt the Treaty talks."

"I would be honored, sir. I have had the pleasure of meeting Captain Branscombe, and I don't believe she had anything to do with the terrorists. And of course I am familiar with Inarrii dress and custom, so I am not inclined to believe any incorrect behavior, or at least according to Inarrii custom." He grinned.

Asler caught the quick hint of affection in his tone and knew the man was thinking of his own new Inarrii wife, the first official coupling of the two races.

The tight feeling in Asler's chest began to ease for the first time in days. Salis rested a hand on his back and Asler took a deep breath.

"Very good. Let's go." Finar nodded and signaled the transfer bubble to activate, encircling the four men for quick transport to the ship Horneu. In moments the transfer was complete, the human officer barely staggering as they emerged.

"Examiner Kiis and Fiiten, please take Major Brown to communications level one and have him report in to his commander. I will be informing our Council of the current situation, and then we will call for an emergency meeting at the Treaty Center on the Earth Base." He reached for Asler's shoulder, gripped him hard. *"Be ready, Asler. You will need to conduct a display of m'ittar publicly. You will have to display your memories of working with Susan. You will be examined and your relationship to her...it may end here. It will all depend on what we can reveal. Be prepared."*

"Examiner Kiis, as a matter of record, until after this hearing, you are deemed to be in the care of Examiner Fiiten. He will be conducting all inquiries."

"I understand." Asler nodded to Jannii and Salis. His back stiffened despite the fact that he knew this was the only way. It was take the chance of ending his career or risk Susan's sanity. There was no choice.

ONE THING SUE remembered clearly was being burned. The memory stood out where many others seemed blurred. Some of that was what she and Asler had done to her memories by reviewing them the way they had. But she knew that some of it was her mind playing tricks on her, wiping out what wasn't healthy for her to see. She knew that, but it didn't stop her from resenting the fact.

She paced the small room she'd been given during the inquisition. Inquisition seemed an appropriate term, filled with the possibility of violence and not necessarily the truth.

At least it wasn't a dank dark room on the junker. She'd made it out of that, survived if nothing else. *Don't believe it. You and Asler have discovered something important out of all that pain. Something that will help your world.* Sue berated herself. Wall, wall, bed, toilet, sink—Sue paced the room again. *Why didn't he come?* Thoughts of Asler competed for attention and were thrust aside. *He didn't come because he couldn't.* She believed he would be there if he could, she *had* to believe in what they had found together, even if they hadn't said the words aloud.

Her councilor, who'd been suspiciously silent over the last day, had finally told her what was happening. The Starforce Intelligence Department had taken control of her case. Things were going from bad to worse—first the Confederacy had investigated, then the human council, and now she'd been passed on like a hot potato to the SID. The newly created agency had already achieved a ruthless reputation.

Sweat formed cold and clammy down her back. She hadn't been warm since she'd left the Horneu. *And that thought brings me right back to Asler.* Sue shook her head and sat on the narrow bed.

"Attention, Officer on Deck." The guard at her door announced as the door slid open to reveal Base Commander Davies.

He smiled at her, but she couldn't bring herself to return the welcome.

She slowly stood to attention. The tilt at the corner of his lips faltered and disappeared.

"Captain Branscombe. You look well."

"Sir."

"Everything will be fine, Sue. Just do your duty, answer the questions. You'll be fine."

"May I be frank, sir?" she asked. Her throat threatened to close in on the words as anger aligned with resentment.

"Yes, yes of course." He seemed to be at a loss for words, surprise and dismay making the lines on his face deepen. A new experience for him, she guessed.

"How could you? How could you tell the SID that you found me half naked on board the Horneu? You don't even know what was going on. You didn't even ask. For years I thought of you as a father, someone I trusted. But you didn't ask me what was happening, you just made assumptions and jumped right in. Now you want me to 'do my duty'? My god, I've been captured, tortured, assumed to be a traitor. Then, when I worked to actually discover something that could help our world, you come in acting like I am an unsupervised and oversexed teenager?"

"I…I…" Davies stuttered over her revelation. "The SID? What do you mean?"

"The SID have taken over my case, apparently."

He turned from her, sat heavily on the bed. "I had no idea it would come to this. I'd…heard some things about the Inarrii, and I thought…I thought you shouldn't be coerced, or pushed into something after you'd been treated so badly. I just wanted you here with our people. I thought you would be safer."

Sue took in his drooping shoulders and worn face. She believed him. This was the man who had taken her under his wing. Of course he'd wanted to protect her.

She sat beside him. "The problem is, I can't answer their questions. I'm in big trouble, commander."

"I don't think I can get you out. It was all I could do to get in here to see you."

She swallowed. "Can you get a message to Asler Kiis? I…I don't think he can get me out, but I'd like to tell him —I'd like to tell him I love him."

Davies's eyes widened in surprise. "You love him? He isn't human."

"I know. But it doesn't matter, and I don't care. They are so like us, and I can feel things with him that I never felt with anyone else. He helped me. He helped me to admit that I was so afraid I would do anything to get away from the torture, and he helped me to see that what I did was my only choice when I told them where the meeting was." She closed her eyes. "They almost broke me. I got to the point that I wouldn't even try escape when it was possible, I was so afraid."

"Can't you tell the SID that?"

"You know it won't be enough. They need someone to blame, and it looks like I'm all they have."

"What about what you said, about discovering something that could help?"

She sighed. "I don't know that the SID would believe me. I can't prove what I saw. I can't even remember seeing it, just what Asler says we witnessed."

Davies shook his head. "It won't be enough."

"No. Only the Inarrii will know what to do with the information anyway."

They sat quietly for a moment. There was nothing left to say. She leaned slightly against his shoulder. It was the only comfort she could have from him, a man who'd meant so much to her but was still only her commander. The buzzer sounded, and her cell door swung open.

"I'll pass on your message," Davies whispered as he rose.

Sue watched him leave. Her heart sank as she wondered if he could get through to Asler, or if it would really matter.

ASLER GRITTED his teeth as he watched Susan march into the room, a guard at her back. Their eyes met across the room.

"Asler!" Surprise and delight tinted her mental tone as she greeted him silently through *m'ittar*.

He pressed his lips even more tightly together as delight turned to confusion on her face when he didn't answer. She didn't know—he *couldn't* answer.

The rules of the Confederacy were clear. They'd made their case for an interruption in the Treaty talks. The weight of two Examiners, along with a commander and the human ambassador, had been enough to ensure they could present their case, but he was now in the care of another Examiner. Outgoing *m'ittar* was not allowed, not even when the attending Examiner Advocate was a friend.

Salis gripped his shoulder in warning and in support, even as the thought passed through Asler's mind.

"I must take objection to this meeting and remind each of you that Captain Branscombe is in the custody of the SID." The Starforce Investigation officer had risen to speak to the room at large. The Human Council sat on one side of the room, their treaty meeting table abandoned in the need for a larger audience, and the Confederacy officers sat on the other. A Confederacy projection platform had been erected at the front of the room, its low stage a circle of hope—at least to Asler.

Admiral Jeffers rose from his seat. Asler hadn't seen him since the last meeting, but he knew Jeffers led the Human Council and had been officiating at the Treaty talks. "Your objection has been noted, but the reason for this meeting outweighs the SID objectives." He motioned to Commander Finar. "Please continue, Commander."

"As I was saying, your honors, our method of investigation differs wildly from yours. Our *m'ittar*, or mind speech, has deeper abilities in some of our people. Our Examiners in particular have the ability to review memories and pass judgment on motive, as well as retrieve valuable information. This was explained when Examiner Kiis took control of the investigation in to the first attack against the Treaty."

Murmurs passed though the crowd. "First attack? Have there been others?"

"There have." Finar walked to the front of the room, standing before the platform. "As the attacks were directed against the Confederacy base and our ship the Horneu, it was agreed that until the investigation was complete, more information would not be passed on. More interruptions to the Treaty negotiations are not needed as I am sure you will all agree."

The SID officer stood again. "No, we would not agree. This is exactly whey the SID should have had control of the investigation—you admit that you are hiding things from us."

"Sit down," Admiral Jeffers barked.

"Please, if I may continue." Finar spoke quietly, and the room fell silent to hear each nuance of his words. "This does involve all of us. Perhaps it was wrong of the Confederacy to keep silent on the subject of the attacks. But there is a further piece of information you must be made aware of. The Confederacy has long been troubled by members of a group we call the Ravagers. Destructive pirates of planetary resources, the Ravagers follow at our heels to snatch up and devour what they can grasp away from our protection. We feared they would be nearby, planning on attacking the Earth if for some reason the Treaty failed. Now we have proof that what we feared is true, and that the attacks have been instigated by them, been made more effective by their technology."

Once again the SID officer stood. His skin had flushed to a livid purple. "You claim we must join with you or we will be attacked? I say you've likely staged these attacks yourself to force us to agree quickly to whatever terms that you have set."

"We understand your doubts. We are prepared to prove everything."

"With more alien technology? With more lies? How can we trust your proof?"

"We ask that you watch and listen to what we can offer as proof, and we ask that you consider that we did not need to offer this information. We could have let you interrogate an innocent woman, let you break her mind. We could have kept silent on the attacks and let the course of the Treaty make its way, one way or another. We do not need to protect your world. We do not have to have your agreement. But we have come to know some of you, and we have come to hope that we can be partners within the Confederacy."

"Sit down, officer. We will listen to the proof. And," Admiral Jeffers gestured to the door, "if you cannot control yourself, you can leave."

Finar continued as the SID officer sputtered in his chair. "This platform is a *m'ittar* projection device. It will allow you to see the memories being reviewed, and the methods we use. Examiner Salis Fiiten will conduct the first examination."

Salis stood, and Asler followed as he led the way to the platform. Asler's heart raced. If Salis slipped only once and exposed a memory from a previous investigation, both their careers would be in jeopardy. If he exposed anything incorrect about his relationship with Susan, her trial might continue, despite what they could prove about the Ravager involvement. And if any of that came to pass, his chances of being with her again were gone.

"Physical contact is necessary for *m'ittar.*" Salis addressed the gathering. "Between Inarrii, where mind contact is common, only mild touching is necessary to access the memories by a skilled Examiner."

The watching Admiral made a motion with his hand, catching Salis's attention "Yes?"

"May we ask questions during your examination?"

Asler looked at the floor and worked to keep his face expressionless. This would make things even more dangerous. External influence could affect the choice of memories being reviewed.

"You can ask now, or immediately after, but not during the actual memory being played out. I must have quiet to concentrate. As you might imagine, the mind is a delicate subject, and Examiner Kiis has put his career at risk by offering to be publicly examined. If his memories are distorted or secure information is revealed, he will lose his position, both within the Confederacy and within his personal clan. Today he risks everything for the truth." Salis looked out into the audience, but no further questions were posed. He laid one hand on Asler's forehead, sliding his fingers against the roots of Asler's hair and brushing the flat *L'inar*. *"Are you ready?"*

"Do I have to be?" Asler opened his mind for his friend. *"Be careful in there."*

"We are initiating contact." Salis slid his other hand around the back of Asler's neck. The platform hummed beneath his knees. The room faded to an opaque grey. Then Susan's face appeared before him with her luscious lips wet and parted, her skin flushed from his kisses. Her eyes glazed and he glimpsed himself sitting beside her on his office bench. He watched as he and Susan leaned closer together, his hands wrapping around her biceps, and recognized their stance as a *m'ittar* pose.

From Asler's perspective, he watched again as they reviewed the first memory of her torture. How would Susan feel about watching the memory she'd been so glad to lose? Now she would have it again, although without the pain, thankfully. She and the rest of the audience would watch what had happened to her as though it were a three dimensional vid. As though they watched hologram actors playing out parts on the Confederacy stage.

The memory faded, and was followed by one of his own, saving the injured diner and watching Susan beat down the fire in the dining room, risking her life to help save the men and women aboard the Horneu. He admired her again—her bravery, her beauty. There was no escaping this; his feelings were going to be revealed as clearly as though he said them aloud to the watching audience. There was no lying in *m'ittar*, or even hiding emotions. This was part of the risk to his career.

Salis moved on to the next memory he'd shared with Susan. A second interrogation, and torture, and the revelation of the Gathan technology. As he watched again the glow from the alien device, he sensed Salis withdraw from his mind. The grey field surrounding them dissipated, the viewers becoming clear. He and Salis had moved into a close embrace. They drew apart as Commander Finar stepped forward.

"This is the proof that you needed, gentlemen. The device you saw around that man's neck is clear indication that the terrorist group Terran Purity is working, albeit unknowingly, with the Ravagers. And I think you will also agree that the information Captain Branscombe revealed was under extreme duress."

Admiral Jeffers nodded and appeared to be about to speak when the SID officer broke in again. "What kind of proof is this? That man," he pointed to Asler, "has developed a relationship with Captain Branscombe. Of course he is going to review the memories that favor her actions. And how are we supposed to know that a shiny necklace is some sort of advanced Alien spy technology?" He sneered as he spoke.

Asler glanced at Susan. Her face appeared more pale than usual, but the glint of anger and determination in her eyes assured him she was going to recover from seeing herself tortured once again. Asler stood. "You have my word as Examiner that these memories are accurate, and that Captain Branscombe is completely exonerated. Commander Finar can present more proof on the technical aspect of the Gathan device."

Admiral Jeffers stood. "I accept your word, Examiner Kiis. Thank you for your expert testimony." He turned to face Susan, sitting only two rows from him. "Captain Branscombe, you are released from custody. You may return to your base."

"But—" the Starforce agent tried to interrupt.

"The SID are relieved from the case. You are dismissed." He ignored the rage on the man's face.

"Actually, Admiral Jeffers, I would ask that Captain Branscombe return to the Horneu for further examination and therapy," Finar requested. "She may still have memories that can help identify the attackers, and she needs to be under the care of a therapist for the emotional stress and pain she has undergone."

Asler listened in surprise, his heart thudding loudly in his chest. This was more than he had hoped for. The quick fire of heat flashed along the lines of his *l'inar*. He wanted her, needed her with him. He stared at her, trying to catch her eyes, but she kept her gaze firmly on the floor.

"Captain Branscombe? Would you be willing to undergo further questioning?" Concern edged the Admiral's voice.

Asler held his breath as she hesitated. What could she be considering? Was she unwilling to face her memories again, or had he been wrong about her feelings for him?

"Yes."

WHAT THE HELL did I agree to? Sue asked herself the same question again. She'd been freed, and here she was back on board the Confederacy Ship Horneu, assigned to go over memories that she never, ever wanted to think about again. Asler hadn't wanted to acknowledge her before the Treaty officials, wouldn't even answer her, let alone acknowledge that they'd had any relationship. Part of her knew it was for her own good as well as his own that he hadn't, but still it rankled that he hadn't defended her in a more personal way. She didn't want to discover that what she felt for him was only in her mind, that he respected her or admired her but didn't feel anything more. That it had really been only sex.

So why was she here?

She drummed her fingers against the heated cushions of her seat and startled when they responded with a soothing vibration. The Confederacy had a council meeting going on behind closed doors, and despite asking her to be here, they had not included her in whatever they were discussing now.

Just as she was about to rise and pace the tiny waiting room, the doors slip open and Examiner Salis Fiiten waived her in.

"Captain Branscombe," Salis introduced her to the table of seated Inarrii. Nearby, an empty stage like the one that Salis had used to project Asler's memories to the Treaty officials. Asler stood to one side of the stage, his brilliant green eyes intent on her.

Sue sucked in a quick breath at the sight of him, his bronze skin exposed except for there the *pettan* covered him. His *l'inar* seemed darker than ever, and he seemed to be struggling to keep them flat. The thought had her blood heating, her cheeks flushing. Whatever the reasons for his earlier actions, he desired her, at the very least.

"Ahem," Salis caught her attention.

"Sorry," she sent to Salis. A gasp came from one of the Inarrii, and she realized with a start that they had heard her apology. If anything, she flushed harder.

Salis addressed the gathering. "Captain Branscombe has agreed to review her memories with us. However, as you have just experienced, she has developed strong *m'ittar* capabilities. I feel that it will be necessary for her to continue to work with Asler Kiis on this, even though he is no longer an official Examiner."

Sue stiffened. "Why is Asler no longer an Examiner?" she demanded.

"Despite the precautions we took at the Earth hearing, Asler Kiis has been relieved of his position for allowing his memories to be exposed," Salis explained. "While we know that there was a very urgent reason, there is no help for it. Confederacy Law dictates he must abandon his career."

"What? I can't believe it! He saved the Treaty!"

"Yes, and for that reason, he has been offered a position with Earth, in a new role as Ambassador. He will also be helping you sift your memories for clues, as well as recover your recent ordeal." One of the Inarrii, a gentle-looking old man, spoke mind to mind with her.

"We have one difficulty. Until Asler has a sufficiently shielded area on your Starforce Base, he must work here. But to work here he must, as a non-Examiner, have you give permission with witnesses to *m'ittar* contact."

Sue hesitated. Asler had shut her out at the Treaty inquiry, and had kept silent about their relationship. Did he avoid it because he believed her reputation would be damaged? Or because he didn't want to commit formally to her?

She looked again at him. He stood completely still and silent, only his heated green eyes and the ripples in his *l'inar* conveying anything to her. But she couldn't hide her feelings for him.

"Yes, I want to work with Asler Kiis."

"Please join him on the stage and initiate *m'ittar*, and indicate that you agree." Salis touched her gently on the shoulder.

Sue walked to the stage, her eyes intent on Asler. Reaching for his hand, they stepped onto the stage together. Her heart raced, and a shiver passed through her at the heat radiating from his skin. She lowered her eyes to his chest to see the *l'inar* ridges rising to attention before her.

"Susan, are you well? I can feel your pain. I am sorry I couldn't free you earlier." His thoughts caressed her and she realized

she could feel the emotion behind them, nearly taste it now in a way she hadn't before.

"You gave up your career to prove I was innocent. Does this mean you lost your clan as well? Is that what they meant at the hearing?"

"It doesn't matter. The truth is revealed, and you are free. That's all that matters."

Her heart pounded. He really had given everything away for her. This was the moment she had dreamed of for the last few days. She had to know how he felt, even if it meant exposing her feelings first. *"I love you."* The thought raced from her mind.

"They can hear you, Ya'lenali."

"I don't care. What does that word mean?" She leaned in, laid her face on the bare skin of his chest.

"It means 'my heart, my love.' I love you." His mental voice grew ragged as she began to lick the hard ridges of his *l'inar*. *"You must stop that."*

"No, I must not. I love you. I give you permission to initiate m'ittar, to work with me to look for clues about the Ravagers. I agree to your help, and ask for it willingly." She worded the permission as carefully as she could, even as she licked and traced the path of his *l'inar* down his chest. Keeping her mind on two things was more difficult than she had thought.

"I heard that too." Asler laughed into her mind.

Behind her, she caught the sounds of chairs sliding out from the table. She glanced back, and the old Inarrii grinned and waived at her.

"Wait, I thought I had to do this in public. You know," she insisted to Asler, "Like in the dining room."

Salis laughed from the doorway. *"M'itta lensahn is a private thing. Congratulations, and welcome to the Confederacy."*

Sue frowned at the closing door. "What is *M'itta lensahn*?"

"More than marriage. It is a permanent mating, a joining of souls. Do you still want to keep licking me like that?" Hope and desire tinted his mental voice.

"Oh, yes. I love you, Asler Kiis. Treaty be damned. This is a contract between our hearts."

She couldn't wait, didn't care that this was a public room or that there was no time to find a ring. She knelt on the platform, her heart pounding as he joined her on his knees. She reached out her hands to touch his chest and the thick ridges of his *L'inar.* *"Ya'lenali..."* she stumbled over the word slightly. "My heart. I love you, and I don't care what the future might bring, as long as I spend it with you."

He slid his hands over her smooth skin until they rested against the nape of her neck. *"Inar tel sahan yowlenaii. Ya'lenali* I will teach you all I know of *m'ittar,* and I will learn all I can from you as well. I will always love you."

He pulled her to him, kissed her. Carefully he began to caress her, tracing patterns against her skin. She moaned, his touch both arousing and frustrating as he explored her neck, her shoulders, her breasts. In return she began to stroke his *L'inar,* following the tightening skin with her fingertips and then her lips, finally licking them . His skin tasted of the same scent she'd associated only with him.

He trembled as she licked the whorls of ridges surrounding his left breast. Encouraged she traced them further down his abdomen. "Gods woman, you are killing me."

"Someday soon we will talk about your gods." She returned his earlier words to him. "But for now, *Ya'lenali,* you will just have to grin and bear it."

His soft chuckles turned to moans as she grabbed the edge of his *pettan* and yanked it down. His cock sprang into view, the ridges circling it defined for her viewing pleasure. She wet her lips, and he moaned in anticipation. A coil of feminine satisfaction curled through her. He was completely at her mercy.

"Lay back and let me enjoy you, Asler Kiis."

Immediately he dropped down to the platform to comply. As his naked skin touched the platform she realized it was still active. Around her, above her, she saw and felt his memory of their last lovemaking. It was her turn to groan. His emotions, his pleasure, no, *their* pleasure combined pulsed all around them.

She looked back at him saw the love reflected in his eyes. Slowly she lowered her mouth to the crests at the base of his cock. She licked them, followed them until she reached the tip of his cock and they were both panting with desire. His eyes locked with hers as she took him into her mouth.

With a long pull of suction she made her final, silent promise to him. She would please him, just as he would pleasure her, for the rest of their lives.

Unable to wait, to slow anything down, he shuddered uncontrollably and called out her name as his seed spilled inside her waiting lips.

A moment later she was in his arms again and experiencing his pleasure and love as it reflected from him around the projection platform. It was surrounded by this intense pleasure that he lay her down and peeled her *pettan* from her body. Inch after inch he caressed her, touching and stroking until she could not concentrate on anything *but* his touch. In seconds he had her naked and spread open before him, his fingers caressing her clit, her helpless moans seeming to drive him on.

He brushed her most sensitive spots until she could take it no longer and cried out his name. Before she could fully crest the peak of her orgasm, he rolled on top of her, pressing his cock against her wet heat. Slowly, one ridged section at a time, he drove into her, thrusting until their rhythms matched, from the sounds of their panting breaths to the beat of their pounding hearts.

"Ya'lenali." The word whispered from between their joined breaths, and they were one.

Afterword

A Note from the Author About The Inarrii Language

One of the things I loved most about the Inarrii was their language. I've spent some time creating a phrasebook so I could remember from story to the next, and found myself interested in their spelling, grammar, and syntax (so sue me, I'm an editor when wearing a different hat and name).

Here are a few (in order of appearance not alphabetically) from the first two books, expect this list to grow:

Inure – one race of the Confederacy

Chammis – very soft woolen material – ie ceremonial robes – somewhat heavy

Pettan – short legged covering that wraps from waist to knee

Kahemnit dal – a casual swear like shit

Tel sho ahoi – SOS signal

Tel sho ahoi sho amnetii – sos ship down

Sho Amnetii Gohan yi – ship self destruct.

Sinaa – Inarrii equivalent of a vagina

Saiin - Inarrii equivalent of a penis

Inar tel sahiir – A formal greeting between Inarrii meaning roughly "the world's welcome to you"

Commander Jannii Finar – commander of the Jupiter Moon outbase on Europa

Sterali – a couch that moulds to shape, is meant to eat on and make love on

Yessin – noodle dish

Rothan – a wine like beverage

Saiithan – long cylindrical cookies – light, like almond cookies in taste, made from pressed cheese like substance instead of nuts

Tel sahiir denay – formal goodbye

Pet-horin - winter pajamas

Inar tel sahan yowlenaii – a more loving greeting meaning loosely - welcome to our world together, always.

Ya'lenali – my heart – my love

M'ittar densah – form of mind contact that allows the person in the memory to step out of it to review it

Gathan – blue skinned race of bipeds that was rejected by the Confederacy and has joined with the Raveners. They have darker blue glands that change color in reaction to fear.

M'itta lensahn – ritual mating – roughly marriage in a private ceremony

Slam – a drug that increases stamina, speed, even speed of thought, but makes you itch till you bleed and makes you mean everything you say

Tocuh – a type of touch seal

Ya'sai lenali - asking a lover for more – begging for more – asking for more pleasure

Lin'thal – soul

About the Author

Lilly Cain is a wild woman with a deep throaty laugh, plunging necklines and a great lover of all things sensual – perfume, chocolate, silk! She never has to worry about finding a date or keeping a man in line. She keeps her blond hair long and curly, wears beautiful clothes and loves loud music. Lilly lives her private life in the pages of her books.

All of the above is just so much silliness. When not living up to her pen name, Lilly lives in Atlantic Canada, although she spent eight years in Bermuda, enjoying the heat and the pink sands. She returned to her homeland so she could see the changing of the seasons once again. When not writing she paints, swills coffee and vodka (but not together), and fights her writing pals for chocolate (true story).

Lilly is a single mom who loves reading and writing, dabbling in art and loving and caring for her two daughters. She loves romance in all of its varying heat levels. She loves the chilling moments and the humor in her novels as much as the steaming hot interludes. Her stories are an escape and a release, and she hopes that they can give you that power, too.

To contact Lilly and to find out more about her books, reach out to her website at http://www.lillycain.com

Coming up next? *Undercover Alliance - Book 3 in The Confederacy Treaty Series* Releasing in ebook format September 1st, 2020. Check Lilly's website above for dates and links.

Also by Lilly Cain

If the love story in Lilly Cain's *Alien Revealed* swept you away, don't miss her other high heat books! And, catch a sample of book two, *The Naked Truth*, at the end of this book!

Read a sample of book 3!

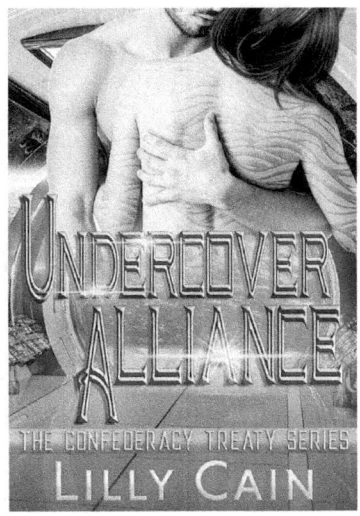

Chapter One

"You've got company," Davis's tense voice called through the comm unit.

"No shit." Starforce Special Agent John Norton glanced down at the hull of the ship. The metal still glowed red where it had been struck by laser fire only a few feet away from his position.

John tracked the small fighter skimming close to the long hull of the Starship *Osprey*. Its dark metal body nearly matched the blackness of space. It was coming back for another shot. Twisting, John fired his hand laser. It sheared through the vacuum of space and pierced the edge of the attacker's hull. Dodging return fire, he leaped for the communication array pod at the far end of the ship and hoped like hell his aim was good and his magnetic boots would clamp, or he'd be hurtling into space like garbage. Since no one was going to admit he was even on board, there was no chance of rescue. His heart pounded, his breath rasping loudly inside the confines of his polarized helmet. He turned and fired again. This time the laser hit a crucial spot, and the small craft peeled off from its attack course.

John released the laser, allowing it to dangle from his wrist strap, and gripped the ship as his boots hit and clamped tight to the edge of the array. Leaning into the small amount of shelter provided by the communication pod, he scanned above him. Only one sleek, little fighter had gone for him, its design confirming what he'd already been told. There was more to the terrorist group Terran Purity than a ragtag group of human racists. The fighter was too sophisticated to be of Earth origin. The *Osprey* hadn't picked it up, or Davis would have caught that on the online chatter. That meant the attacker had some serious shielding. The terrorist shouldn't have detected John either—a single moving figure on the exterior of the massive human Starship *Osprey*, his suit designed to deflect not only the coldness of space but any heat or ultrasonic detection. At least, that was the plan.

Quickly he flipped open the closest access panel and toggled the manual relay on the communications pod. Two more minutes and he would have the fourth and final bug in place. Not that he could rely on the listening devices any longer. No one in Starforce should have known he was here, let alone the Purity assholes. Someone could be aware of the surveillance equipment he was planting as well. Any information he got from them would be suspect at best. He pulled the bug from his forearm pocket and pressed it against the console. He felt it dissolve into the circuitry through the pressure-sensitive fingerpads on his suit and suppressed a shudder. It never failed to revolt him the way the damn bugs could work their way through anything electronic, and he vowed again to refuse the microcircuit brain implants the brass had been pushing on all upper-level agents.

Motion flickered in the corner of his eye. Instantly he snapped off the magnetic clamps in his boots and shoved away from the array. Laser fire bit into the hull inches away from where he'd been locked on. He fired the narrow jets on his back, the silent explosion of compressed gas propelling him away from the array and back toward his only exit without a hint of heat to give away his location. The fucking fighter was back, its maneuverability amazing as it followed him across the underbelly of the ship.

John grabbed at his dangling laser and flicked a shot across what he guessed was the view panel of the pilot. He snapped the magnets back on his boots, slamming into the hull. The fighter's momentum pulled the ship past his location, and he shot the laser at full capacity, directly at what had to be a rear power nodule.

In a flash of light, the back of the fighter ship ripped forward through its front.

John gasped. An explosion was not what he'd expected. The resulting shockwave flashed toward him, driving him back against the hull in a way that made him twist and shout out in sudden pain. Then the blackness of space claimed the final charred remains of the attacker.

Panting for breath, John weighed his options. His knee radiated agony. There wouldn't be much time before someone came to investigate the explosion. The *Osprey* captain would already be aware of the attack, although hopefully not what had caused the terrorist ship to detonate. They'd be looking for answers. John straightened and forced himself to bring up his helmet comp unit and signal for a map. It flared to life across his visor, the light color of the map illuminating his screen with a sudden flare of pain behind his eyes. The explosion had left his head throbbing and his knee feeling as though he'd been kicked, hard.

"Fuck."

"I heard that, Norton. Good to know you're alive. Now get your ass in here."

"I'm working on it, Davis. Keep your pants on." John's map pointed the way and a quick pulse from his jet pushed him toward the closest service hatch.

"Trust me, I wouldn't go anywhere near you without my pants." The deep voice of his mission tech radiated good humor. The man had a sick sense of what was funny in the middle of the most dangerous of missions. If it wasn't for John's strict rule—no partners—he might have taken the man out for a few drinks and laughs. But keeping things professional and separate had saved his ass more than once. Connections only made things more complicated.

"I keep telling you, Davis—you're not my type."

"Far as I can see, you haven't got a type. And you have three minutes before the security team reaches that hatch. Move your ass."

John didn't reply. His knee throbbed now with every heartbeat. In space he didn't have to put his weight on it. Inside the ship it was going to be a bitch to put any speed on and avoid arrest by the very people he was actually protecting. He had to get back to his cover assignment. He reached the hatch and yanked it open. Davis would have already triggered the lock release from wherever the hell he was, via remote link. Now would come the hard part.

Soryen Sarina Tariim slammed a fist into the oral port of her charging attacker. The lean alien went down in a graceless collapse, only to be replaced by another, and another. They swarmed her, their stinking, slimy skin repulsive as they tried to push her to the soggy ground and rip her limb from limb. She grabbed one creature's arm and slammed him into the next, kicking a third in its midsection. Still more of them darted toward her. All they had to do was pull her breather from her face and she'd be dead in minutes. Around her other Inarrii fought hand to hand against the Archat swarm. Lasers were useless and actually dangerous to fire in the methane-rich atmosphere of this world.

She'd lost her first set of *dash'tet* knives and now reached for her second, grabbing for the hilts strapped to her calves. The movement cost her; two more Archat were on her in seconds but she rolled with their attack, using their momentum to skewer them through on her long *dash'tet*.

A long hooting howl sounded as she pulled her knives from their bodies. The unprovoked attack on the Inarrii scout party was now a retreat. Inarrii all around her raised their voices in a ragged cheer, and she laughed aloud.

Too soon, the feeling of exhilaration melted away. Her grin faded. This was useless. There was no real victory. She didn't know the Inarrii warrior who had battled only a few feet away. He wasn't her teammate and this wasn't real. With a decisive slash of her *dash'tet*, still dripping with alien gore, she shut down the battle simulator and stepped out of the holo unit. Her battle gear faded as she exited, but the bruising she'd received inside the simulation remained painfully real.

Fighting these images, these pale reflections of old battles, provided only a few moments of relief from the truth. She'd been there, on the very mission this simulation had been based on. She'd fought on dozens of worlds, performed hundreds of dangerous missions. But it would never be the same. She rubbed the upper muscle of her left arm, felt the damage no Inarrii medtech would ever be able to remove.

Beneath the fading scar tissue was the real injury. Her *L'inar* were severed, the damage far deeper than surface lacerations. Despite a dozen reconstructive surgeries, her synapses no longer meshed. She would never again have complete release, experience the utter sexual abandon the sensitive *L'inar* nerve lines could inspire. And without that completion, her mind was at risk. At least, according to Inarrii belief.

Her therapist said she would recover. Her commander agreed. Her clan was sympathetic, but already garnering the political credit and honor points from a permanent disability of one of their own in the line of duty. Her current assignment indicated her clan was more in touch with reality than either of her advisors.

Sarina exited the simulation lounge of the Inarrii flagship Horneu. This would be her last evening on board before she headed to her new assignment and complete boredom. There would be no more laser fights in her future, no space battles. With a groan, she walked to the next section of the training level. The familiar and usually comforting scent of sweat in the strength focus room did nothing to cool the anger that burned inside her over her predicament. She could fly a ship, strategize and fight with the best, excel at everything a warrior could hope for, but she would never get the chance to prove it again. Just because her damn *L'inar* and her lack of a sex life were a supposed threat to her sanity.

"Fuck." She tested the human curse and found it vaguely satisfying, and in her situation the curse was ironically apt. She moved over to the resistance boards and attached the wrist and ankle straps. Throwing her weight and her anger into the workout, she pushed herself to the limit.

The boards hummed with power as she strained to touch them, to press them past her usual level. Sweat beaded on her back, slowly slipping down the length of her spine. Her *L'inar* reacted to the slight touch of the drops of liquid. Sensation fizzled along the nerves, flared around the curve of her ribs, bounced erratically around her abdomen to flicker over the lower curve of her breasts, only to dissipate. She jerked in her restraints, the sensation an erotic tease, a reminder of the fact that she hadn't had sex in a month and wasn't likely to experience it any time soon.

She ripped the bands from her wrists and glanced around the room, thankful the area remained nearly empty. Perhaps they were right. Even if she managed to reach orgasm again, these unpredictably odd flashes of *L'inar* activity just might drive her insane. At least no one had witnessed her strange reaction. One set of warriors trained in hand-to-hand combat in the far corner of the training level. Their strikes and parries nearly blurred in rapid progression. They were in sync with each other, even their breaths matching rhythms. Sarina pulled off her ankle straps, never taking her eyes off the sparring couple. They had to be a couple. If they weren't, they soon would be. The flashing blows were slowing, becoming more of a dance than an attack. Before the night was out, they would be wrapped in a dance of a different kind. Skin on sweaty skin.

Sarina sagged against the resistance boards. Their power had disengaged the moment she pulled off the tethers. Inert now, they bowed slightly with her weight. Perhaps leaving the Horneu wouldn't be such a bad thing. Despite the incredible boredom of guarding a human nobody, at least on the human ships there was

no open sex. No erotic displays, no direct offers that held the
intimacy of *m'ittar* mind contact and a promise that couldn't be
fulfilled—complete *L'inar* arousal and release.

She turned away from the couple and walked quietly from the
room to the sonic cleansers. The hum of the cleansing units
passed their vibration up through the soles of her feet and into
her body. An ache low in her belly reminded her again, as if she
needed any more reminders, that it had been weeks since she'd
shared the tension-relieving experience of sex. Without sex,
Inarrii could not de-stress.

That was the reason she was being assigned to bodyguard such a
low-status human. What would they have done with her if she
hadn't already learned standard English? No de-stressing meant
an eventual breakdown, but how much stress could she
experience guarding John Bennings, a lawyer who spent his days
deep in the tangled webs of information completing the final
layer of the human/Confederation Treaty?

It was a horrifyingly dull thought.

Still, a job was a job. And as long as she could, she'd retain the
rank of warrior, a *Soryen*, giving every assignment everything she
had. Anyone who said she couldn't could…fuck themselves. She
snickered at her own sick sense of humor and then leaned into
the sonic cleanser.

"Special Agent Norton, your mission is simple. Continue with
your cover as John Bennings, midlevel lawyer and contract
specialist. We'll feed you all the documentation you'll need to
work your way through the negotiations, but as the inside man
you will be the final line against these terrorists. This Treaty must
go through. Earth needs this agreement. It hasn't become
common knowledge yet, but with your clearance you must be
aware of the alien forces we've been tracking throughout the
system." Commander-In-Chief Johaness motioned toward the
information displayed across the room.

John rotated in his seat to observe the vid panel on the
conference room wall. The seamless flow of information across
its microthin surface wasn't new. He was aware the Inarrii
weren't the only nonhumans in the area, but it was surprising

that information on the number of craft now visible on the outer edges of the galaxy wasn't spread across every news vid on the planet. There were a lot of them, far too many. These had to be the Raveners that the Inarrii had warned would follow in their wake, looking for any undefended planet whose resources were up for the taking. They were moving in, faster than anyone had expected, at least according to the scrolling data.

John turned back to the CIC. She was a tall, thin-boned woman, almost raw in her severity, but the commander-in-chief held more power than most people could dream of. Their eyes met.

He made a slight nod. "The terrorist group Terran Purity—they are still confirmed as the driving force behind the recent attacks on the Inarrii and the negotiating boards?"

"Yes, but intel from several sources has indicated that the Raveners, in particular the Gathan, a high-tech race rejected by the Confederacy and probably bearing a grudge, have been secretly supplying Terran Purity with advanced firepower." She nodded at the screen, where a picture of a blue-skinned being flickered across the surface, followed by several weapons schematics. "Your recent spacewalk confirmed it."

John studied a nasty-looking laser cannon. "That could rip a hole right through a shuttle."

"Exactly." The CIC slid a small metallic item toward him. "This is a little something new of our own. A portable force shield. I hope you don't need to give it a trial run any time soon."

John picked the tiny generator up, noted the thumbprint and DNA control on the end. They would have already keyed it to his pattern. That they would give him a prototype defense item underlined the gravity and the danger inherent in his mission. "You expect further attacks."

"Yes. Intel has indicated not only increasing frontal assaults of the type we've seen over the last month but also more insidious strikes against the negotiation personnel of both the Inarrii and the human contingents." She snapped off the vid and turned away, taking her seat behind the huge mahogany desk against the back wall of the conference room. "There are only two steps left before the Treaty is complete. The Human Accord—the agreement of every major human political party to go ahead with the Treaty—and the Treaty signing itself." She rubbed the back of her neck, a rare expression of worry and a real measure of the increasing danger.

"While we've taken every precaution, upgraded every level of security, we know there'll be more attacks, and that some may succeed. But no one will be aware of your presence. No one but myself and your immediate commander. You'll be there, standing shoulder to shoulder with the men and women who are building our future in the galaxy. You'll ensure that they've got their chance."

John stood. "Understood." He turned to leave but she caught his attention with a small sound, the simple clearing of her throat.

"Special Agent Norton. One last thing. The Inarrii know nothing of your position. But your cover, along with every other human legal representative, has been assigned an Inarrii bodyguard. They, like us, are taking no chances."

John nodded. The complication was minor. "I'm sure they've done what they see as aid for us without completely taxing their resources. A bodyguard is not a problem."

"Let's hope not, Agent. There can be no distractions, and no interference with your mission."

First impressions could say a lot about a person, but observation of a subject when he was at ease, following a routine he was familiar with, told far more. Sarina studied her charge carefully as he worked. The meeting had been in session for an hour since the last intermission. She'd been introduced briefly to John Bennings by the captain of the *Osprey* during their meal break. Benning's handshake had been firm, and his height and muscular frame belied a life of facts and figures. With his powerful, lean muscles, his body spoke more of the strength brought on by hard exercise, perhaps even some human form of hand-to-hand combat. It also spoke softly, seductively of sex.

His hands were long-fingered. He wore a well-tailored white shirt and dark pants, but he'd turned back the cuffs on his sleeves almost to his elbows. Fine, light brown hairs along his exposed forearms caught her attention and held it as she considered where else he might have such silken decoration. He wore the hair on his head short, not like the long locks of a male Inarrii warrior. But there was something about the way he carried himself. He reminded her of someone.

"And that's enough for today. Thank you everyone. We'll meet again tomorrow." The human chairman stood up from the meeting table. "I'll remind you that we have two weeks until the next meeting of the Treaty negotiation boards. We've been making good progress, but there is still a long way to go to finalize the agreements on Earth before the signing of the first Intergalactic Treaty." He smiled, but clearly the rest of the team had been dismissed.

The lawyers and legal aids began shuffling about, most packing up their datapads and styluses or tapping shut their coms. Not Bennings. He sat still as the rest moved on as a pack, the humans and their unobtrusive Inarrii guards. She watched him watching them until her gaze caught his attention.

He studied her and she returned the look. His eyes were a soft gray, not blue or brown like the few humans she'd met so far, and no where near her own verdant green, the most common Inarrii color. His eyes were beautiful. And it didn't matter.

She broke the connection and looked around the room, scanning the exits and the few people still within the area.

"Sergeant Tariim." He used the human equivalent of her Inarrii rank of *Soryen* and he spoke softly, but she caught the deep timbre of his voice beyond its hushed tones. "I'm beat. I'm going back to my quarters. I won't be going anywhere, so you can stand down. Get settled in. I'm sure they've quartered you somewhere near my rooms."

He'd gotten close to her without making a sound. She'd been aware of his movements, but if she hadn't been paying attention, would she have even noticed that he'd stepped closer, let alone come within striking distance of her? *Interesting.* Even the spongy shoes most humans wore on board ship usually made some noise. Their height was close; she looked directly into his eyes without shifting her stance. A quick flicker of awareness passed over her. For an instant she wondered if he could have some form of *m'ittar*; it was common knowledge that some humans had proven their ability to share thoughts and emotions, at least to some degree. This is what made them such attractive possible members for the Confederacy.

"Actually, I have had our rooms reassigned. Our quarters are now on the third deck, sector two." She stated the fact and ignored the flash of attraction that raced through her as she inhaled his muted scent. He smelled of fresh rain along the beach line of her home world. Like an ocean breeze.

"Reassigned." His eyes took on a steely note. "You've had our rooms reassigned together? As in, sharing the rooms?"

"We have adjoining quarters. I cannot guard you from the opposite end of the ship. I will not be…settling in. My shift doesn't end until the Treaty is compete and I am transferred."

For a moment she thought he might argue with her. A tiny line of tension formed along the corner of his full mouth. She took a quick breath as the old excitement flickered through her muscles. A fight would be good. A little excitement on a surely boring tour of duty. Perhaps if it became physical they would send her back to the Horneu. *And what would you do there?* a silent voice whispered within her.

But he broke off eye contact, lowered his gaze to flicker briefly over her body before he nodded. "Fine. I'm sure you know what you're doing."

He'd deferred to her. A strange feeling of disappointment settled into her stomach. She shook her head and led the way out of the conference room and through the corridor to the ship's central lift. What did she think a data-shuffling tech would do, challenge her for dominance? Maybe she was already beginning to lose her mind. She needed his compliance if she expected to protect him. In a dangerous situation, she had to know he would follow her lead. She considered the slight hesitation, the line of tension beside his mouth before he'd accepted the room change. Perhaps he would follow her. Perhaps not. As long as it didn't get to that point it didn't matter, and after the mind-numbingly boring meeting she'd just observed, surely no one would be interested in attacking this level of tedious bureaucracy.